The Motor City Chronicles

Short Stories of the 1920s

J.A. Jernay

Paper ISBN: 978-1-960936-02-8

Plotworks Publishing

Visit Plotworks Publishing to sign up for our newsletter and to purchase more titles by J.A. Jernay, A.J. Renwick, and others.

The Bootleggers

DETROIT, 1927

When Edmund Grabowski learned that his wife was pregnant for a fifth time, he grew quiet.

"Say something," said Millie.

"No."

"Then sit down for dinner."

"I'm angry."

"Just have dinner. We'll talk about it."

He sat down at the bare table. His four other daughters were already arranged around the table. Each had a bowl and a spoon. Outside the window, a light snow was falling. The radiator hissed and clanked.

Millie carried a heavy iron pot from the kitchen and placed it in the middle of the table. Edmund looked inside.

"Cabbage soup," he said.

"I can't buy the city chicken until it goes on sale."

"When does it go on sale?"

"Wednesday."

"I don't have money until Friday."

She said nothing to that. Edmund looked at the faces of his four daughters as his wife served the cabbage soup. They were slurping, the faces staring down into their bowls.

"My bowl is cracked," one whispered to her mother.

Edmund pointed a finger at her. "You have your own bowl."

"Yes."

The finger moved to the next daughter. "And you too."

She nodded.

He went around the table. All yeses.

Edmund threw down his spoon. "Four children," he said, "and four bowls." It doesn't make sense.

"Why papa?"

Edmund suddenly stood up. He walked into the kitchen and unhooked the large dipping spoon they used to dip into the pitcher. It was hanging on a nail in the wall next to the sink.

"Don't," said Millie.

Edmund put the dipping spoon in the middle of the table. None of the girls were eating now.

"Give me your bowls," he said.

"I'm not done," said one.

"Dump the soup back into the pot and give the bowls to me."

The girls poured their soups back into the pot. Scared eyes met each other, seeking reassurance.

"Now stack them," he said.

One of the girls stacked the bowls.

"Slide them to me," he said.

It was done. Their father lifted the stack of the soup bowls and threw them across the room. They bounced against the wall and fell to the floor. The bowls rocked back and forth until the last one finally grew still. Silence slowly crept back into the room.

"We need to share," said Edmund. Does everybody understand that?

"I liked my bowl," said the littlest one.

Edmund summoned all of his patience. "You can have a dipper for a few seconds. Like this."

Edmund filled up the slim dipping spoon with soup and passed it to the littlest one. "Use this to take some soup and then pass it on."

The daughters began to pass the dipper around the table.

"See," he said, "it's like the line at the Rouge. We each have a few seconds to do our jobs before it moves on."

"Will it come back?" said the littlest one.

"Of course it will," he said. "Here it is now. Dip in— that's good. Sip from it. Now pass it along."

The dipper circled the table from hand to hand. A spoon was dipped into it at each stop. Round resentful eyes watched him.

"What," said Edmund.

"You're not using the dipper," said Millie.

He looked down at the bowl and spoon. "I make the rules."

He sat there, regarding her. Then he lifted his bowl to his mouth and slurped the last of his soup. When he was finished, he stood up and walked to the door.

"I'm going out," he said.

"Don't," she said.

"I'm going out," he repeated, taking his coat.

* * *

Edmund buried his chin into his coat, tilted his cap down over his face, and stamped down the street.

His black hobnail boot kicked a mound of gray slush on the sidewalk. In a few hours it would be a mound of ice. Edmund disliked ice. It made him think of the old country.

He turned off Joseph Campeau and down a side street. Dark tenement houses crammed the sidewalks, their second-story bedroom windows close enough for neighbor children to slap hands. He quickened his pace.

He stopped at a house at the end of the block. Its front porch was unswept and the interior appeared dark. Edmund squinted his eyes. Behind the house, at the end of the driveway, was a garage. A large man stood beside it, a hulk of a shadow in darkness. The orange tip of a cigarette poked out from his face like a heated branding iron.

He stomped up the driveway. He came up to the man by the garage and took a deep breath and stood up to the man. The man was a head higher. The orange tip of his cigarette fell onto the brim of Edmund's hat.

"You let me in," said Edmund.

"Why," said the man.

"I been here before and Mister Cuppers knows I'm tight."

"Maybe I remember you."

"Okay."

The man blew smoke into Edmund's face. "Maybe that's why I'm not letting you in."

"Maybe you'd like a punch in the gut."

The man flicked his cigarette into the snow and seized Edmund by the lapel of his coat. The fabric was scrunched into his hammy fists. Then he lifted Edmund three inches into the air.

"Set him down," said a voice.

Edmund looked over his shoulder. It was a thin, hawkish Polack chewing on his lower lip. His eyes were intelligent and quick.

"Mister Cuppers," said Edmund, still dangling.

"I know my name."

The beefy doorman lowered Edmund to the ground. Then the doorman lit a new cigarette and stepped aside as though nothing had happened.

"O'Malley," said Mister Cuppers.

"Yes sir."

"Don't harass this man."

O'Malley blew a wreath of smoke into the frigid air. He didn't say anything.

"See," said Mister Cuppers, "Edmund suffers from many troubles. For instance, he has a lousy personality. But we let him in anyways."

"Thank you," said Edmund, brushing off his coat.

"Of course."

Edmund entered the blind pig. O'Malley watched him, his face like a smashed jack o'lantern.

The garage held fifteen people if they stood sideways at the bar and all drank with their right hands. The tight space wasn't unwelcome, given the cold drafts that came gusting between the planked walls. Body heat was the unspoken reason for the garage's success in the winter.

Edmund found a place at the bar and watched Mister Cuppers behind the counter, pouring whiskey into each shot glass as it emptied. He owned a small pharmacy on Joseph Campau that he ran during the day. Inside his mind was a powerful ledger that was always keeping score and he was one of the few men to take advantage of any opportunity that presented itself.

Mister Cuppers walked over to Edmund and plunked a glass tumbler onto the counter. It was still sticky from the last person who'd drank from it.

"What're you pouring?" said Edmund.

"Canadian Club," said Mister Cuppers.

"I don't like whiskey."

"What do you like?"

"Vodka."

"We don't have vodka. We have whiskey."

"Anything else?"

"We have whiskey."

"All right then."

He poured a shot and watched Edmund throw it back down his throat. He poured another, then quickly placed his hand over the glass before Edmund could take it.

"So," Mister Cuppers said, his eyes dancing.

"So," said Edmund.

"I've got a business proposition."

"Okay."

"Edmund, you're going to make a lot of money tomorrow night."

"Doing what?"

"Come outside."

"But I just got here."

"We can't talk inside."

He motioned to the many pairs of ears that were listening to the conversation.

"Oh."

It was a clear black night and a white moon hung in the sky like a communion wafer. The snow crunched under their shoes as they tramped into the middle of the backyard.

"Some important friends have asked me to find a driver for a very lucrative mission," said Mister Cuppers.

Edmund looked at him blankly.

"That means profitable," said Mister Cuppers. "You'll get paid."

"What do I gotta do?"

"Do you have an automobile?"

"No."

"Can you find a man who has one?"

"Yeah."

"Find that man and I've got something for you tomorrow night."

"Okay."

"But it's only tomorrow night. Don't come back here in a week looking for it."

"Okay."

Mister Cuppers regarded him, his fingers drumming on the whiskey bottle in his other hand. He hadn't dared to leave it inside.

"Is that all?" said Edmund.

"You come back tomorrow with an automobile, tonight's drinks are on the house."

"Okay."

"If you don't come back tomorrow with an automobile, then you don't come back here at all. Understand?"

"Yeah."

"Let's go back in. I'll set you up."

Over Mister Cuppers' shoulder, the smashed jack o'lantern face leered at Edmund.

* * *

"Hey Joey," said Edmund.

"What," answered the man.

They were sitting next to one another on the streetcar going to the Rouge. It was six-thirty in the morning. Edmund was wearing the same hobnail boots as the night before and his hat was still pulled over his eyes. Over his shoulder was a satchel with his bagged lunch that Millie had made. It contained two boiled potatoes and a stale dinner roll.

"You still got that Tudor?"

"Of course."

"But you don't drive it."

Joey shook his head. "It's hard to steer after work with my arms hangin like a pair of cutlets. And this way I can sleep here."

"It doesn't work, does it. The Tudor."

Joey furrowed his brow. "It works, buddy. No reason to lie. Fact, I took it out this Sunday."

Edmund grinned. "Don't get sore."

"I'm not sore."

"You want to make some money?"

"That depends," said Joey.

"On what?"

"The nature of the work."

"I don't know the nature. But we need your automobile."

"Let me think about it."

"There's no time. It has to be tonight."

"Oh."

Edmund and Joey sat side-by-side, swaying slightly, hearing the clanging of the streetcar's wheels as it rolled along its tracks.

"Okay," said Joey finally.

"You're in?"

"Yes."

"Bring your automobile at five o'clock tonight to St Florian's."

"The Polack church?"

"Yes."

"Okay."

They sat in silence on the wooden bench until the streetcar arrived at the entrance of the Rouge.

* * *

At five o'clock that evening, Edmund stood shivering under a streetlight. Behind him towered the front façade of St. Florian's.

A *putt-putt-putt* sound turned his head. Coming down the street was a beautiful new Model T. It had custom-made side panels.

The Tudor pulled up in front of him. He opened the side door and stepped inside. Joey was dressed to the nines.

"Looks like you're going to the Pontchartrain."

"I've just got to match the automobile, that's all. Where are we going?"

"To the pharmacy on Joseph Campeau."

Joey put the car in gear and they slowly motored two blocks away.

"Park here," said Edmund.

Joey obeyed, then shut off the engine. They stepped out of the car and walked across the busy street to a pharmacy. The sign in the window read *CLOSED*. Edmund knocked on the glass. Inside, Mister Cuppers stood on his tiptoes and craned his neck. Then he came over to the door and unlocked it.

"Come in," he said.

Edmund and Joey stepped inside.

"You're the man with the automobile," said Mister Cuppers.

"That's me," said Joey.

"Welcome. I want you to make a delivery."

"Oh boy," said Joey.

"It's very important. If you fail, many powerful people will be unhappy."

The two men didn't say anything to that. Mister Cuppers' huge eyes were magnified by his glasses.

"We need you to run some whiskey over from Windsor."

"I knew it," said Joey.

"Knew what?"

"Bootlegging. I ain't crossin that bridge with a trunk full of hooch. That's a twenty-dollar fine."

"You won't be crossing by bridge," said Mister Cuppers.

"Then how we gonna cross?"

"By ice."

Edmund thought about it. Joey caught his arm. "I see people do this," he said. "They drive right up over the river up into the garages of them Grosse Pointe mansions."

"There's more to tell," said Mister Cuppers.

"Go on," said Joey.

"You'll be part of a caravan. Twenty cars. We've got the whole police department looking the other way for two hours."

"I thought the smuggling was all done by boat," said Edmund.

"Not when it's frozen. The Christmas season is almost upon us and we need to replenish the stores. If you're dependable, there'll be two or three more runs before the spring melt."

Mister Cuppers noticed their hesitation.

"Don't say no."

"How much do we get," said Joey.

"Fifty dollars."

"Let's do it," he said.

They both looked at Edmund.

"All right," he said.

* * *

Two hours later, the pair had crossed the bridge into Windsor. In Canada, the sale and consumption of alcohol had not been prohibited, and distilleries had sprouted along the riverbanks like mushrooms, all selling illegally to the Americans.

Edmund and Joey motored down the quiet, darkened Canadian streets, the vehicle jouncing underneath them.

After twenty minutes of moving north along the river, they found the warehouse in Walkerville. The words *Hiram Walker* were displayed above it.

Joey pulled the car through an open sliding door and found a line of cars already waiting inside the dimly lit warehouse. A fellow in a heavy coat swaggered over, slapping the sides of his thigh with a newspaper. He bent down to the unrolled window.

"You're driving *this*?"

"It's my car," said Joey.

The Canadian looked quizzically at him. "You couldn't find no jalopy?"

"I didn't hear nothing about a jalopy. But I cleaned out the back to make some room."

"Son, you're not stockin' it. You're pulling it."

The man walked away, still slapping the newspaper against his thigh. Edmund watched him go.

"How are we gonna pull it?" Joey said.

"I don't know."

A minute later, the automobiles at the front of the line rumbled to life. They circled around and drove past, a parade of Model Ts, corroded, gimpy, a decade old. Flinty eyes squinted at them through cracked windshields.

"You got the nicest car here," said Edmund.

"Shuddup," said Joey.

Their turn came, and Edmund followed the line back down to the riverbank. Under a string of lamplights, the boats were already lined up at the edge. Each was covered with a canvas tarp, and each was outfitted with a pair of skis underneath. Each car in the caravan was backed up to a ski-boat. Then a group of three men hitched the boat to the rear of the vehicle.

"So the hooch is in the boat," said Edmund.

"They don't care about the car," said Joey.

"Nah."

"It don't matter if a car goes in the river. The hooch is in the boat."

They watched the first car slowly pull the boat down onto the ice, two yellow headlights barging straight into the blowing icy darkness. Slowly, one by one, the cars nosed onto the frozen surface, the boats sliding behind them.

"Mister Cuppers didn't say a word about getting a jalopy," said Joey. "What a bum."

"I coulda found one for ten bucks," said Edmund.

Joey drummed his fingers on the wheel, then pulled his knit cap down over his head and leaned against the window.

"I can't do it, Edmund."

"We can't quit now."

"Then let's switch."

"You want me to drive?"

"Yeah."

"Okay."

He and Edmund ran around the car and reentered on the opposite side. Edmund slid behind the wheel.

They waited a half hour in the queue, engine idling. Joey smoked cigarettes and they both looked across the river at the art deco skyline of Detroit, the neon purple and pink and green reflected in the night sky above.

Soon the line of boats had grown shorter. The front of the caravan had disappeared into the darkness and was presumably already safely on the other side.

Finally a man waved them forward. Edmund eased the car down to the river's edge and backed up to the next ski-boat. The distillery workers, disguised by heavy masks, hitched it to the trunk of Joey's car with some heavy rope. Then one came alongside the window and yanked the mask up over his head. It was the man from the warehouse.

"No turning," he said. "Just go straight. The faster, the better."

"Yeah."

"Say it back to me. What'd I just say?"

"No turning."

"What else?"

"The faster, the better."

The man slapped the side panel. That meant go. Edmund shifted into first gear and slowly eased the car onto the ice.

They were on the river, and after the initial bump, they felt no difference between cement and ice. Slowly Edmund increased his speed. Ten miles per hour. Fifteen miles per hour. Twenty miles per hour.

The caravan trekked across the frozen surface of the dark river. Beneath the wheels lay one inch of snow, ten inches of ice, and eighty feet of water.

Edmund kept his grip tight, driving as straight as a Presbyterian. Joey peered out the passenger side window, knitting his fingers nervously.

"We coulda said no," he said. "We coulda backed out. Your boy Mister Cuppers told us the ice wouldn't give."

"He don't give a shit about us."

"We coulda said no."

"You can't say no to the Purple Gang."

"Maybe we coulda."

Edmund pressed the accelerator. Twenty-five miles per hour. Thirty miles per hour. Thirty-five miles per hour. The winter wind curled its long fingers through the cracks of the door frames and shook the entire frame, right down to the chassis.

"I hope the ice holds," said Joey, blowing into his hands.

"It will," answered Edmund.

Straight ahead and growing larger was the Detroit side of the river. A string of lights showed the ramp onto the frozen ground. Five men in mittens and work boots were hauling the handles of whiskey out of the ski-boats and sliding them into the backs of three waiting trucks.

Then the car in front of them halted. The rear end lifted. The front end sank.

It had broken through the ice.

A strangled sound came out of Joey's throat. There was enough light to see that the driver had flung himself out the door and was splashing in the water. His boat was already floating.

"Turn!" shouted Joey.

Edmund twisted the wheel to the right, two whole

spins. The Tudor responded, banking forty-five degrees in an instant.

But the ski-boat tied to the back of the automobile, secured by loose rope, didn't turn. It broke free from its moorings, barreled straight ahead, and collided with the rear of the other boat.

A horrific sound echoed in the cold river air. It was the sound of the bottles inside the boat shattering against themselves.

Edmund stopped the car a safe distance away and they both leapt out of the vehicle. The brown liquid had already begun seeping onto the ice and forming a large pool beneath the ski-boat. The sweet smell of distilled whiskey drifted into the air.

The few cars following them had steered a wide arc around the situation and were already pulling up onto the bank ahead. Now their car was the only one left on the river.

Joey took off his hat and threw it on the ice and stamped on it.

"For Pete's sake," he cried. "We're dead men."

They looked towards shore. It was only fifty yards away. The men from the Purple Gang had seen the accident. They were grouped together, conferring. A few were swinging meaty fists together menacingly. These were goons. They wouldn't care whose fault it was. Somebody had cost the operation money and somebody was going to pay.

At the scene of the accident scene, only the rumble seat remained above water. Meanwhile, the driver of the other automobile had hauled himself out of the water and was staggering back across the ice plain, clothing already frozen, towards Ontario. That was the best option, to his terrified mind.

Joey was looking at Edmund with an odd expression. His nostrils opened and closed.

"We got to run," he said.

"I'm not going to Canada."

"Me neither."

"Then we're going to Grosse Pointe."

Joey ran to the driver's side door of his Tudor. Edmund threw himself into the passenger seat. The engine rumbled to life.

Joey pointed the car parallel with the riverbank and shifted quickly. Soon they were racing northeast, up the river. Edmund looked to the shore. To his left, driving parallel with them underneath the streetlights of Jefferson Avenue, were two other automobiles.

But they weren't alone. Edmund turned around and saw two pairs of lights on the ice behind them. The goons.

"Drive faster," he said.

"This ain't like driving on a road," said Joey. "God help us but this is a disaster."

The headlights grew larger behind them.

"If we make it to Grosse Pointe the cops might help us," said Joey.

"You really think that?"

Joey didn't respond.

Soon the humble bungalows to their left had ended, and the baronial estates had begun. Along the riverside ran Lake Shore Drive, a smaller but equally wealthy cousin of the same name in Chicago. Edmund watched the long front lawns, the white pillars, the butlers silhouetted in sober windows.

"Get up onto land," he said, "and quick."

"I need to find a piece of sand."

"Hurry up."

"I'm trying. I don't want a kick in the teeth."

A short beach appeared on the left. Joey quickly wrenched the wheel towards it, and the Tudor careened up over the rough, crusty edge of the frozen riverbank and onto the frozen sand. Then the automobile came to a sudden stop.

The wheels had become bogged down in the frozen sand.

Joey pressed on the accelerator. The engine whined higher. The wheels spun uselessly.

"Dammit," he said, "dammit to hell."

"Look," said Edmund.

Along Lake Shore Drive came a police car. On top of its roof was strung an odd set of wires like a harp.

"What is that on top?" said Joey.

"It's a radio."

"What's it do?"

"It lets the pigs on the streets talk with the pigs in the station."

"No shit."

Behind them, the headlights were growing larger. Twenty seconds lay between them and a month spent with their mouths wired shut. Joey and Edmund leapt from the car and ran across the frozen beach up to Lake Shore Drive. They stood in the street and jumped and hollered and waved like a couple of lunatics.

The police car slowed to a stop. The door opened. A short deputy emerged with a sneer on his face.

"Hiya bud," said Joey. "We're in a load of trouble."

"That ye are," the small cop replied.

His partner's door opened. A very tall man stood up. He

had bulging muscles and was wearing the deputy's badge like an afterthought. He had a face like a smashed jack o'lantern and held a billyclub in his hand.

"They aren't police," whispered Joey.

"That's O'Malley," said Edmund. "He works at Mister Cuppers' blind pig."

"Mister Cuppers is part of the Purple Gang," said Joey. "And this guy—I know him too. He used to work at the Rouge for Mack Bennett bustin' heads."

"And now he's a cop? I'm confused."

"Maybe he just crushes whoever pays him enough."

The small cop sized up the duo with a cold eye. "Word has it, there was a bit of a problem on the river."

"We don't know about that," answered Joey.

"Oh, I think you do."

The pursuing car had pulled off the river and had parked beside the Tudor. Four men piled out. The headlights from both cars were now shining on the two disgraced whiskey runners.

"Dammit," whispered Joey, "what we do?"

"Fight," said Edmund.

O'Malley approached the duo, cracking his knuckles.

"Mister Cuppers said don't give me no trouble," said Edmund. "Remember him saying that?"

"I don't work for him tonight," said O'Malley.

The goon pulled back and delivered a crack to the jaw. It was dense with force. Edmund stumbled backwards on his heels and fell to the ground. Then the goon turned to Joey.

"Get out of here."

Pissing scared, Joey ran to his Tudor, climbed inside, shut the door, and started the engine again. He revved it over and over, the tires spinning uselessly in the sand. He pounded on the steering wheel and screamed.

The four men from the Purple Gang walked up to his Tudor, yanked open the door, pulled him out, and threw him onto the beach.

"That's his tough luck," said O'Malley. "I didn't see them boys. You?"

"Naw," said the small cop. "I don't see real good. You could say I'm blind at times."

Edmund and Joey were thrown side by side on the ground. O'Malley, the small cop, and the four members of the Purple Gang all circled around them and began kicking.

Up on the road, they found Edmund unconscious the next morning. His body was covered in bruises and his jaw was swollen so big that he was forced to drink soup for the next three months.

A rounded spoon wouldn't fit in his lips, either, so he had to use the dipping spoon.

The Department of Sociology

The carpet knife drew a neat line of red across the back of Edmund Grabowski's left hand.

He dropped the tool and swore under his breath. It'd been a single catch in the fabric. The knife had jumped, slashing his left hand, which had been holding down the upholstery.

He wrapped a dirty rag around his hand and studied the dark wood highchair. It was plain, its slightly curved arms and legs the only concession to the modern style. Half the seat was covered with the black fabric, and a bag of goose feathers in the corner awaited stuffing.

Edmund pushed out the makeshift door. It was tiny shack in the backyard, attached to the privy. The winter wind played reluctant music through the branches of the trees. Edmund didn't listen to it. He crunched across the dirty snow and went back into the house.

* * *

A cold boiled potato with salt awaited him at the kitchen table. In the living room was his wife, Millie. She was sitting near the radiator, a thin burgundy curtain spread over her lap and cascading onto the dirty plank floor. She was tatting. The bare window admitted the light of a gray late winter afternoon.

"Where's the child?" he said.

Millie paused. "Why?"

"Is that a bad question?"

"She's sleeping in the other room."

"She's always sleeping."

"That's what an infant does, Edmund. Now you stay hushed or you'll wake her up."

On the sideboard, Edmund found a bottle of whiskey with less than an inch remaining. He sat down at the table, spread his feet wide, and tilted it nearly vertical into his mouth. Then he tossed the empty bottle onto the floor and wiped his sleeve across his face. He slumped over on the table, head in his arms.

For a while, the only sound in the room was the sound of the needle clicking against the thimble.

Edmund lifted his head. "Four daughters," he said.

"That's correct."

"I must have offended God, I believe."

"Believe it."

"This is your fault, Millie."

Her eyes found his hand. "You hurt yourself out in the shed?"

"A tool slipped."

"Do you need me to wrap it?"

"No."

He stood up.

"You didn't eat your potato," she said.

"I don't want it."

"Where are you going?"

"Out."

Edmund lifted his flapjack hat off a peg near the door and stomped outside.

The front yard was a stretch of mud from fence to fence. Two forlorn chickens pecked for insects. A narrow plank led across the mud to the street. He walked heel-to-toe across the plank and looked back at his home.

It was a working man's house. It had no foundation, no insulation. Its walls consisted of boards set up vertically on the earth. The canvas sheeting stretched over the outside walls rippled slightly in the breeze.

Edmund spit on the ground and walked away.

* * *

As Edmund entered the pool hall, he shook off the cold and studied the place. Twenty other working men were arranged around the three billiards tables. The eyes watched him warily.

"Edmund," one said.

"Kasper," he replied. "There's too many krauts here."

He hung his coat and hat on a row of pegs near the door. A streetcar rumbled by and halted all conversation for a moment. Kasper went to the bar and brought him a glass of ginger ale.

"Here," said Kasper.

"Why the friendliness," said Edmund.

"Well, we've seen you angry. You want something else?"

Edmund sipped from the beverage. "No, it'll do."

Kasper chewed on his lip and surveyed the pool hall. "The krauts aren't too bad, once you get to know them."

"That's your opinion."

"Do you want to play?"

"I do," said Edmund.

"It's a dollar to enter."

"Really."

Kasper pointed to the line of silver dollars on the side of the billiards table.

"This is new," said Edmund.

"Yes, fairly. Don't tell the pigs."

"Why would I?"

"Why wouldn't you?"

Edmund furrowed his eyebrows. "I don't like your tone."

Kasper laid a reassuring hand upon his shoulder. "Now, don't get sore. Are you in?"

"No. I don't have it."

"That's too bad."

Edmund leaned against the wall and watched a man set up the triangle of ivory balls. He watched Kasper dust his hands with chalk, then use the long stick to send the cue ball barreling towards the triangle. A loud crack, and the fifteen balls went careening around the green tabletop.

"Well struck," said Edmund.

"Thank you," Kasper replied. "Are you content?"

"Yes."

"Good. Millie?"

"She doesn't change."

Another streetcar rumbled by, ending the chatter, rattling Edmund's spine through the thin wall. He watched Kasper line up another shot, banking the seven off the three. It went wide.

"Rotten luck," said Edmund.

"Indeed."

Kasper's opponent sunk three shots in a row. Edmund set down his empty glass.

"That's all for you today?" said Kasper.

"No, I'm getting another."

"Ah."

Edmund approached the bar. It was a plank of unfinished wood that had been nailed to four thin legs. The bartender was drying a glass. A small mustache had settled upon his lip like a dead caterpillar.

"One more," said Edmund.

"Vernors?"

"Yes."

The bartender opened another bottle of the ginger ale and poured it into a fresh glass.

"How much?"

"It's on the house."

"Again?"

"We like to keep you happy."

Edmund turned back to the games. He was unaccustomed to this friendliness. Feeling proud, he hooked a thumb into the upper pocket of his vest. He felt something cold and round and hard against its tip. He pulled it out.

It was a silver dollar.

He flipped the coin into the air. "I'm in, boys."

The men at the tables exchanged worried glances with one another. Pausing his preparation for his next shot, Kasper straightened himself and slowly turned to face Edmund. He spoke with great restraint and a fake smile on his face.

"Well then," said Kasper, "bring it over here."

Edmund crossed the room and laid down the coin with the others and picked up a stick.

"You have to wait until this game is finished," said Kasper.

"It's already finished. You're going to lose."

"Stay patient and you'll get your turn."

At that moment, the door to the pool hall burst open. A young boy of no more than nine or ten years streaked in, full of passion. All eyes turned to him.

"Does anybody here work at the Rouge? Does anybody work at the Rouge?" the boy shouted.

Several men grunted yes. Edmund raised his hand.

"It's the Sociology Department," the boy said. "They're going through the neighborhood."

A groan went through the group of men.

"Which street?" said Kasper.

"I don't know but they're goin' down the alleys."

"That means inspections," said Kasper.

"Shit," said someone.

The bartender came out from behind the bar and addressed the group. "I appreciate your all's business, but anyone employed at the Rouge better run home and get things in order, quick."

Eight of the men reached for their coats and headed out the door, grumbling. Edmund watched them leave.

"You have to go too," said Kasper.

He sneered. "Henry Ford can go check up on his own ass."

"It's no joke. They'll cut your salary in half."

"I take care of my family."

"Go home," said Kasper.

Edmund felt a cold, round silver dollar pressed into his palm. He stuffed the coin back into his vest pocket and reached for his coat and left the pool hall.

The door swung shut, and Kasper breathed out. He

collected the stack of silver dollars and took them over to the bartender and placed them on the counter.

"Thanks for the loan," he said.

"My pleasure," replied the man

"How long you think before he catches on?"

"A long time. He's dumber than a fence post."

"Why don't you just ban him?"

The bartender dropped the coins into the till. "It would cause more trouble than it's worth," he said.

Edmund hurried down the sidewalk and turned back towards his house. He saw the rear bumper of a Model A driving slowly down the street, its wheels rolling down the pocked and pitted ground. Then he saw the vehicle stop in front of the muddy yard with the plank.

In front of his house.

"Christ in heaven," he muttered.

Edmund ran up just as the two men stepped out. They wore black suits with high white collars. These were Ford executives.

"Who are you looking for?" said Edmund.

One of the men looked at his clipboard. "The home of a Mister Edmund Grabowski."

"That's my home."

The men regarded him with a gaze that was colder than the air. "My name is Mister Heinz and this is Mister Staub. We're from the Sociological Department of the Ford Motor Company. We're here today to inspect the quality of your home life. May we enter your home?"

Edmund jutted his chin out. He tried to draw himself up to their height.

"Hell no."

"We advise you to answer in the affirmative, Mister Grabowski."

"Why?"

"What is your wage?"

"Five dollars a day."

"We have the authority to reduce that wage to two dollars and thirty-four cents a day."

The bluster slowly leaked out of Edmund like air from a balloon.

"Fine then," he said.

"Would you like to alert your wife that we'll be entering?"

"Why?"

"In case she's indecent."

"She's never indecent."

"Do you have any infants?"

"A girl."

"She could be feeding the girl."

Edmund walked away from the tall German men in their black suits and high collars. He didn't dare turn his back on them. The back of his boot heel caught on the lip of the plank and he tripped backwards and fell in the mud.

"Are you okay, Mister Grabowski?" A smile decorated Staub's face.

"I'm well."

He lifted himself up from the ground, stumbled down the plank, threw open the door, and stormed into the house.

"What happened to you?" said Millie, looking at him.

"Get dressed."

"What happened?

"The Sociological Department is here."

"Oh no."

Edmund went to the sink and washed the mud off his clothing.

"Right now?" she said.

"They're outside."

Millie put down her tatting and stood up from the rocking chair with one hand underneath her back. She went to the bedroom and closed it tightly.

"They'll wake her up," she said.

"Listen to me, Millie. I don't drink."

"Yes, you do."

"You're not understanding me. I don't drink."

"You don't drink?"

"I stopped four years ago. With the law."

"Okay."

"Understood?"

"Yes."

She collected the empty whiskey bottle from the floor and stuffed it under her skirts.

Edmund went back outside. The two German executives were standing by the door of their Model A, their feet spread wide, their hands clasped behind their backs.

"We're ready to get this over with," he said.

Mister Heinz and Mister Staub walked in single file across the plank towards the house.

"Did you construct this yourself?" said Mister Heinz.

"I did."

"It's ingenious."

"It's a plank."

Mister Heinz managed to summon a smile. "Just trying to make this more pleasant," he said.

* * *

They entered the home. In the kitchen, Millie was standing at the sink, washing dishes.

"Hello," she said. She turned off the water, wiped her hands on her apron, then clasped them together nervously. "I'm Millie."

"My name is Mister Heinz and this is Mister Staub. We're from the Sociological Department of the Ford Motor Company. We're here today to inspect the quality of your home life."

"Is this common?" said Millie.

"Indeed. All Ford employees must undergo such evaluation."

"Why?"

"Because Mister Ford believes that a productive home life translates to a productive factory."

"What do you want here?" said Edmund.

"We're looking for evidence of thrift, cleanliness, and sobriety."

"Oh my," said Millie.

"Don't look so worried, Missus Grabowski. We've already done some checking up on you."

"What've you found?" said Edmund.

"We've looked at your bank account deposits."

"How?"

"Your bank is owned by the Ford Motor Corporation."

"Oh."

"It's nothing to worry about. We found that you've been making weekly deposits."

"I take care of my family," he said.

"Well, that's what we're here to ascertain."

"What does that mean?"

Mister Heinz ignored the question. Instead, he went to the window, noted the bar over the window.

"No curtains?"

"I'm repairing them," said Millie. "They're over on the chair."

"How does your husband treat you?"

"Well."

"Has he ever struck you?"

"Never."

"How many children do you have?"

"Four."

Mister Heinz counted chairs with his finger. "There's only five seats," he said.

"The youngest doesn't eat at the table yet."

"Right. She's the infant. Have you picked out a name?"

"Not yet."

"What do you call her?"

"The baby," said Millie.

Mister Staub sat down at the table and removed a pen and an index card from his pocket.

"I would like to make a list of household debts," he said.

Edmund blew air out of his mouth. "All right."

"Do you have a list I can see?"

"I don't."

"How do you track your debts?"

"In my head."

"Perhaps then you could tell them to me."

"We owe forty-two dollars to the grocer. We owe thirteen and a half dollars to the medical clinic. We owe six dollars and twenty-five cents on the table and chairs."

Mister Staub copied each line onto his index card. "Nothing else?"

"No," said Edmund.

"That's fifty-one dollars and seventy-five cents in arrears."

"How do we know this is the truth?" asked Mister Heinz.

"You can ask them all. I can give you their names."

The two executives from the Sociology Department exchanged nods. That was a satisfactory answer.

"May we see where the children sleep?" said Mister Heinz.

"If you'd like," replied Millie.

She escorted the man to the bedroom. He looked inside.

"Only one bed?"

"Yes sir."

"For four children."

"Three."

"Where does the baby sleep?"

"In our room."

"May I see it?"

Millie opened the door to the master bedroom. Its condition seemed to satisfy Mister Heinz. He strolled back into the main room.

"Mister Grabowski," he began, "I'm going to now ask you a very serious question and I expect a very serious and truthful reply."

Edmund was leaning against the wall near the front door with his arms crossed, still wearing his winter coat.

"Go on," he said.

"Do you drink alcohol?"

A rueful smile crinkled the corner of Edmund's mouth.

"No," he replied.

"Never?"

"Not since they took it away."

"That was four years ago. You haven't had a sip since then?"

"I have not. That would be illegal."

He held the man's eyes. He was a player of the game, as were they.

Mister Heinz tapped his pencil on the clipboard. "Well done," he said.

"Thank you."

Mister Staub turned to Millie. "Do you have any single male boarders?"

"No."

"Have you ever welcomed a single male boarder?"

"Yes."

"Why would you do that? You have daughters in the home."

"It was when we had only the one."

"Isn't that a terrible example for her?"

"She was sixteen months old and we needed the money."

That seemed to satisfy Mister Heinz. The two visitors gathered themselves near the door. Mister Staub cleared his throat. "On behalf of the Sociology Department of the Ford Motor Company, he said, we have concluded that you maintain a fine, moral, Christian home."

"Thank you," said Millie.

"Likewise," said Edmund.

"As a result, it is our recommendation that you keep full wages. Have a good day, the both of you."

Mister Heinz and Mister Staub bowed ever so slightly. Edmund opened the door for them. He watched them cross the plank over the mud, then shut the door.

"That is a relief," said Millie. She reached under her skirt and pulled out the empty whiskey bottle.

"I forgot about that," said Edmund.

"I didn't. It was on the floor."

A sudden knock on the door startled them. Millie looked out the window.

"It's him. He's back."

She shoved the whiskey bottle up her skirts again.

* * *

Edmund opened the door again. It was Mister Heinz. "I'm sorry to disturb," the visitor said, "but may I use the privy before we leave?"

"It's in the back," said Edmund.

"Yes, I'm aware. Thank you."

The man disappeared around the side of the house. Edmund waited until he heard the door of the privy close. Then he came outside and stood on the plank. Mister Staub was already inside the Model A, the engine running.

Edmund watched the door of the privy. When it opened, Mister Heinz emerged with a handkerchief over his nose.

He paused, looking at the flimsy door to the shed next to it.

"And this?" he said.

"It's my work shed."

"Lovely. May I look inside?"

"It's your day."

Mister Heinz opened the door and peered inside the small workspace. "You're building a chair," he said.

"A highchair for the baby."

The visitor reached inside and pulled out the black upholstery for the seat. "What type of fabric is this?"

"I don't know the name."

"Where did you purchase it?"

Edmund blinked repeatedly. "At the textile shop," he said.

"Where?"

"On West Grand Boulevard."

Mister Heinz walked towards him, holding the upholstery. "This is Ford upholstery. This goes on the seats of Ford automobiles."

"No, it doesn't."

Mister Heinz grew very serious. "I'm going to check for a textile shop on West Grand Boulevard. And when I find one -- if I can find one – I'm going to ask if they sell this type of upholstery."

"That's up to you," said Edmund.

A fire burned in Mister Heinz's eyes. "You almost slipped through our fingers, Edmund."

He shook his fist at Edmund, then walked past him into the waiting automobile.

After they'd disappeared down the street, Edmund dropped his head.

"Shit," he said.

* * *

The probation notice arrived four days later. Edmund intercepted the mail before Millie could see.

He took it into the work shed and sat down on the stool. He couldn't read, but he knew what the numerals $2.34 meant. He'd heard about this process from other workers.

Six months' probation at drastically reduced wages.

"Shit," he said, balling up the paper.

Factory Vs College

At the dinner table, Frank Pappas set down his fork, seized with a coughing fit. His large, round frame shook, and his eyeballs bulged as his lips formed a small ring and blew air out into his linen napkin.

Lydia, his wife, came around to the back of his chair and worked circles into his meaty upper back with her hands. The eyes of their three teenage children stole furtive glances from behind their pieces of baked chicken.

The coughing stopped. Rosa's hands continued their duty.

"There, there," she said.

"Forty-nine years on this earth, I never got sick," he said.

"Things change, dear."

"It's the carbon monoxide. Too many years working downriver."

"Maybe you can see about changing jobs. Your brother said they still need help driving streetcars."

"Are you kidding me? That crap doesn't pay."

Lydia moved away from him. "That wasn't what I meant," she said.

"I like the men at the Rouge and I'm not leaving."

Frank pushed up from the table and went to the refrigerator and opened a bottle of German lager. He poured it into a ceramic mug and went outside onto his porch and settled down in his favorite outdoors chair. It had been built from a large wooden spool that a cousin had nicked off a construction site. Frank had sawed off a piece of each circle so it would sit flat. He could afford a better seat, but mostly he liked watching passersby smile when they spotted it. It had personality.

Frank sipped the beer and bathed in the yellow rays of the evening sun beaming through the green boughs of the Dutch elm. His life was good. His bungalow was no different from the thirty-nine others on this block. It had flush toilets. The house came with a small patch of grass in the front yard. Just two miles away was the maddening crush of downtown, but it was pleasant here.

A man came walking down the street, a passenger bag slung across his shoulder. He was dressed in a wrinkled white-collar shirt that was open at the neck and a tie that was loosened halfway down his chest. He was younger than Frank and carried himself with a swagger.

"Well, well," said Frank.

"Just the scoundrel I'm lookin for," came the reply.

"You set the fall schedule yet?"

"No. That's why I was hopin to see ya."

The man bounded up the two steps to the porch and swung his hand in a wide arc, meeting Frank's with force. Frank's beer sloshed onto his pants.

"Say, that looks like a prohibited beverage, mister."

"You keep your mouth shut, Jimmy."

Grinning, the younger man dropped into the other chair and set his bag down.

"Nice place ya got here."

Frank nodded. "Better than that wreck over there," he said.

He pointed at Jimmy's bungalow, across the street and four doors down. It was immaculate and identical to his own.

"Maybe, but either way there's no safer investment than Detroit real estate," said Jimmy.

The older man nodded. "That is the truth, sir."

"Did you catch the fish you were hoping for? The one from Albion?"

"I did not."

"Applesauce."

"You're too old to be saying that, Pappas."

"So Beardsley is throwing again this season?"

"He is."

"What a dewdropper."

"He says he's changed."

Lydia brought out a glass of water and handed it to Jimmy.

"Thank you ma'am," he said.

"Something else?" she inquired.

"No ma'am, I don't partake."

She smiled and left. As the door closed, Frank leaned across the porch and lowered his voice. "Any choice bits of calico this year?"

Jimmy grinned. "Oh, I don't get around the women's fields too much."

"Liar."

The younger man smiled and waved his engagement ring. "I'm cuffed, sir. Now, I have a serious question for you, Pappas."

"That a problem. I left my serious hat at work."

Jimmy drummed his thumbs on his dress pants. "The athletic director is concerned that our student-athletes need toughening up."

"That's probably right. Your university attracts Grosse Pointe softies."

"I know."

"Why don't you use one of the scrub teams? You can call one down from Flint or Battle Creek—"

"No," said Jimmy, "the director wants to help build a culture of Detroit football."

"How so?"

"He wants them to play a team of factory workers."

A rush of air burst out of Frank's mouth. His hand slapped his thigh and stayed there.

"I take it you are surprised," said Jimmy.

"It's a good idea, but the last factory team I knew disbanded even before the war."

"That's why I'm talking to you, Pappas."

Frank looked over. Jimmy was facing him full on. His eyebrows were sending a message.

"You want me to help?"

"You're a foreman at Ford Motor Company, Pappas. How many men do you directly supervise?"

"About sixty."

"How many indirectly?"

"I can reach three hundred or so."

"Could you form a squad?"

"I could. But would I? That's a different question."

Jimmy was on the edge of his seat. "They said you were a fine lineman back in the oughts."

"I was. But it was a different sport then."

"No autopsy, no foul."

"Now, that's an exaggeration—"

"It's true the sport is easier now, Pappas. It's matured."

"Sure. You all have instituted a bushel of new rules."

"So is that a no?"

"No, said Frank.

"So it's a yes."

"What?"

"You said no to my no."

"I'm confused. Anyways, give me time to think about it."

Jimmy stood up. "We're looking to schedule the game the week before Thanksgiving. This would give you over two and a half months to form a squad and practice."

"Okay."

"Let me remind you that you're the one always defending Ford boys as the toughest skull-crackers in the world."

"Yeah, we are."

"So prove it."

Jimmy doffed an imaginary cap and strolled down the steps and went over to his house and went inside. The door closed behind him.

As the sun sank lower and disappeared, Frank stared at the front door of Jimmy's house, thinking.

The next morning, Frank stepped out onto his porch and found a note taped to his door. *Look in the bushes and think about it. -Love, Jimmy*

Frank peered behind the thick bush next to his porch. Hidden in the dark crevice between the greenery and the house were six bottles of German lager.

"Applesauce," he said, tightening his fist.

* * *

Frank charged down the main aisle of Building B of the Ford River Rouge Complex like a hippopotamus on a mission.

He marched through the main aisle of the tool & die portion of the famous factory—the largest in the world—with his customary hard step, his arms pumping like pistons. An unlit cigarette dangled precariously from the corner of his open mouth. On his torso hung an informal beige short-sleeve collar shirt. The points of its lapels nearly touched his shoulders and circles of sweat darkened the armpits.

In his sweaty left hand was a sheaf of flyers.

Frank pivoted right and headed down a short row of equipment. A large young man with a slow face stood in his blue overalls operating a lathe. A pair of protective muffs covered his ears.

Frank waited patiently behind him as the young man finished his task. When it was safe, he tapped the kid on his shoulder.

The young man whirled around. Recognizing Frank, his eyes widened and he ripped off his ear protection. "Yes, Mister Pappas, hello, how do you—"

"You're Luka Kovačević," said Frank.

"Yes, Mister Pappas." His voice betrayed a heavy Croatian accent.

Frank moved the unlit cigarette from one side of his mouth to the other. "Don't look worried, Luka, you're not in trouble. I just want you to play football for me."

"Football," he said.

"That's right, football. I'm organizing a squad, see—and you'd do great."

"How much do they pay?"

Frank shook his head. "No money. It's for fun. Like I said, you'll do great on my team. Big boy like you." He grinned, then thrust a flyer at Luka. "All right here's what you do. Get somebody to read this paper to you. It explains everything. We start next Tuesday at five pm at the fairgrounds on Six Mile Road. Got that? Repeat it back to me."

"Tuesday, five pm, fairground on Six Mile."

"Great. Any questions, ask me next week."

Luka stared at the paper in his hands, confused.

"How're you doing otherwise?" said Frank. "Everything good?"

"They raised the price of the milk at the canteen."

Frank's eyes darted left and right as he processed this comment. "Five dollars a day to an illiterate immigrant and he complains about a seven-cent pint of milk? Whaddya want, a red carpet rolled out every morning for your grand arrival?" His meaty hand smacked Luka on the back. "See ya next week."

The foreman walked away. "Mister Pappas?" said Luka.

"What?"

"Do I really gotta do this?"

Frank surveyed the young man's two-hundred-fifty pound frame. "Yeah, you do."

* * *

At eleven in the morning, Frank began visiting the lunch wagons. A couple hundred of them had been sprinkled strategically around the Rouge complex. At each one, men stood eating fifteen-cent box lunches of ham sandwiches, fruit, jelly, and cupcakes. Some workers held cups of coffee in their hands, chatting.

Approaching one wagon, Frank saw a man sitting cross-legged on the floor. He wore an applejack cap and his face was in his hands. Another worker saw the foreman approaching and nudged the man with his boot.

Too late. Frank was upon the sitting worker in a flash. He crouched down. "You there, something wrong?"

The man lifted his face. Deep hollows under his eyes told stories of inner agony. "No sir."

"Something tells me that's not true," said Frank. "Either way, sitting down is an offense to Henry Ford, the great god of efficiency."

This made the worker smile. "I'm sorry, sir."

He made to stand up, but Frank pushed him down by the shoulder. "No, the damage has been done. See, I'm supposed to write you up now and ruin your life. But it's your lucky day."

"Why?"

The foreman held a flyer in front of his face. "You're going to play football instead."

"Write me up instead," the worker said.

Frank scowled and ignored him. "Question. Can you run?"

"That depends."

"Boy, the only correct answer is yes, or else you'll be in a world of hurt."

"Yes."

"If you run fast enough, I'll let you sit down for all fifteen minutes of your lunch break anytime you want. Hell, I'll even let you lay down."

"I'll think about it."

Frank rolled his eyes. "What's your name?"

"Carl Bernheimer."

He grabbed the worker's badge to check. "Bernheimer, this is not a negotiation. See you next Tuesday."

He patted the worker's applejack cap and moved off. The men nearby turned away, pretending not to hear.

* * *

On his porch, Frank faced Jimmy. "I gotta admit, it's looking bleak."

"How many do you have?" said Jimmy.

"Twelve. Probably thirteen by tomorrow." Frank drank from his ceramic mug and wiped the foam off his lip. "First I tried recruiting directly. Then I tried blackmail, but the others got wise and now everybody's on their best damned behavior. So finally I started sweet talking but all that got me was the icy mitt."

"Soft language is out of character for you," said Jimmy.

"Fair."

They watched the neighborhood children hopscotching in the street.

"There has to be something else," said Jimmy.

"Oh, there is."

"I think I know what you're going to say."

"There's a group that doesn't work in tool & die. A group that contains many excellent athletes."

Jimmy rubbed his forehead. "There would be problems on my end—"

"No doubt—"

"But it wouldn't be impossible—"

"No, not at all—"

"I'd just have to talk to some of the higher-ups at the university—"

"Of course—"

"Three more, Pappas," Jimmy said, "that's all you need."

Frank looked at the horizon, sipping his beer. "We're poking the hornet's nest, and I don't know if it's worth it."

"It will be. Consider this your civic duty for the city of Detroit."

* * *

In the foundry at the Rouge, a group of twenty black men stood assembled around one half of an iron pillar. Their dark skin shone slick with sweat and tones of blue and silver and their large denim overalls were smudged and ripped.

The flyer read: *Wanted: Three Negroes to join football squad. Experience mandatory.* *Promotion to tool & die possible for qualified players.* *Meet Frank Pappas, foreman, here at 3:30 pm.*

Frank himself stood on a catwalk overhead, mopping his face and armpits. He watched the foundry workers motioning towards one another, pointing at the flyer. He saw them jostling another, headbutting, pairs of rams locking horns in a fight for dominance.

"Here we go," he muttered.

* * *

On the floor, the fight started almost as soon as Frank had opened his mouth.

Nearly fifty men had been waiting at the pillar when he'd arrived. Most were strong and tall. Others were slender but were possible runners. Circled around them were a couple hundred of onlookers, smiles on their faces. The scene was backlit by the giant open iron kilns and the circular molds and the orange light cast by the liquid metal within. It was both an industrial hellscape and a cauldron of success.

"Boys," he'd said, holding up his palms, "I only need three of you. If you can't decide upon the three yourselves, then we'll conduct tryouts tomorrow."

A group of onlookers detached themselves from the darkness and strode forward into the light. The group was composed of five white men. Some carried chunks of rebar. None looked particularly athletic.

Frank knew that the foundry wasn't entirely composed of black employees. Some of the unluckier whites—the damaged, the sociopathic, the dumb mutes—were relegated here, to the heat and the darkness and the misery.

"We don't think you need to promote any Negroes," said one.

"We think you should promote us," said another.

A third slapped the rebar against his thigh and jutted his chin out.

The brawl erupted without a word. The white men were surrounded and put on the defensive, driven across the floor, onto carts, against posts. Faces were smashed, eyes gouged, teeth spat out. Soon all five men were on the floor. Some were kicked. The man who'd spoken first was beaten with his own hammer.

Frank allowed the pummeling to go until he was sure that the whites had been subdued. Then he flicked his cigarette away and stormed over, ordering the others to pull back off the whites. Soon the black men were facing him, breathing hard, their faces knotted in anger.

"Drag those white men over here by the pillar," ordered Frank. "Do it."

The black workers dragged the whites by their ankles

across the floor. The five men lay in a pile together, groaning. Frank crouched down and looked at them.

"Is this what you wanted? Is this really how you saw this going?"

No responses.

"Hand over your badges. You boys are getting suspended."

Then Frank stood up and addressed the black workers. "Tryouts at four pm tomorrow, state fairgrounds on Six Mile. I'll post another flyer." Then he looked down at the whites. "And Negroes *only*."

* * *

In the field at the fairgrounds the next day, Frank administered a rudimentary running, blocking, and passing drill for the twenty-two foundry workers who'd showed up. He quickly selected the three best athletes, then thanked the rest individually and offered cigarettes for the streetcar ride home. There were complaints, and several of the rejected players elected to stay and observe.

Nearby stood the thirteen white players he'd recruited earlier. Frank called them over and now, for the first time, were gathered all sixteen members of the River Rouge squad. Some wore stovepipe hats and work boots. Others had come prepared, wearing athletic breeches. Only two had lace-up cleats.

"Welcome," said Frank. "I'm Coach Pappas. First off, this is going to be a serious football squad. We're going to have twice weekly practice and scrimmage games on the weekends. The season will finish with a game against the University of Detroit on November seventeenth. Full attendance is mandatory."

The men stood silent.

"You all have diverse reasons for being here. Some of you have been promised promotions. Some of you were made promises you couldn't refuse. Some just want to succeed at something, for once in your pitiful lives." There was some laughter at that. "How many of you know how to play football?"

Seven raised their hands, including all three of the black players.

"How many know rugby?"

No hands.

"All right. Football is a simple sport and if you follow my instructions, we will become a winning squad." He paced up and down the line of men slapping his clipboard against his thigh. "Firstly, we're all employees of Ford Motor Company and we will represent the company to the greatest extent possible. This means that you will conduct yourselves as gentlemen on and off the pitch. If the Department of Sociology hasn't made a visit to your home yet, you can expect one soon." He lifted a significant eyebrow and looked from face to face to show that he meant it. A few groaned. "So make appropriate preparations, if you know what I mean. Any questions so far?"

No one spoke.

"We all work difficult, physical jobs on the floor at the Rouge. I understand that. So you'll need to take special care of your bodies. That means getting more shuteye and shoveling more food into those big yaps. To that end, I'm speaking with the canteen next week to see about doubling your lunches, no extra charge."

The men grinned. That was music to their ears.

"Also," he continued, "I'm also going to have to ask you to obey the eighteenth amendment. I'm sorry."

Their faces were blank. Frank rephrased it.

"You can't drink."

This caused consternation. "I don't know what you need to get through the night," he continued, "but make sure to keep your hands off the giggle water. Do not get so zozzled, so spifflicated, that you cannot play. If I suspect you have been breaking this rule you will be off the team, and any promise I've made to you will be null and void. Is that clear?"

Silence.

"Is that clear?"

The players mumbled yes.

A black player raised his hand. "Coach, what about uniforms?"

"We don't have any," said Frank.

"So we just play in our street clothes?"

"Yes."

"Seems like we need some uniforms though."

"You handy with a needle?"

The men laughed at this.

Another player raised his hand. "Coach, what's your experience?"

"I played eight years and broke nine bones."

"As a coach," the player said.

"In football, none. But I've coached over six hundred men in the tool & die division of Ford Motor Company."

Bernheimer, slight and sad, raised his hand. "But why are you doing this, Coach?"

Frank pointed at him. "Cheeky one, aren't you? Because I'm a leader of men, Bernheimer."

"You already lead men at the plant," Carl said.

"Well, maybe I just can't get enough."

Carl wasn't finished yet. He eyed the coach. "I think you've got something to prove, Mister Pappas."

Frank looked at him. "You can think whatever you like, Bernheimer."

* * *

They squad rolled as smoothly as a square wheel through its first practice.

To the players, Frank assigned either one of two positions: backs or linemen. The backs were fast and lithe, and the linemen were large.

One back—Greniak, a Polack with a strong arm but no football experience—was assigned to throw the ball. After his fifth wobbly toss fell short, a black player named John Simmons approached to help him.

"See, the fingers go on the laces, see, and then it comes off the fingers in a spiral, see," Simmons explained. "That spiral directs it. See here."

The black player stepped back and threw a perfect spiral to another player twenty meters off.

"That's good," said Greniak. "You should throw the ball."

"No," said Frank. "He doesn't throw the ball."

"I been tossin' those pigskins since I was knee-high to a grasshopper," said Simmons.

Frank shook his head. "You can't, not for this squad."

"But—"

"I know you're good. But the answer is no."

Simmons understood the subtext and said nothing more.

Luka Kovačević cleared his throat. "Coach, why they don't throw the ball to me?"

"You don't touch the ball," said Pappas, "because you're a lineman."

"But I want to catch the ball."

"No, you can't."

"So what I do?"

"You stand in front of Greniak and protect him so *he* can throw the ball to other people."

The Croatian scratched his head and thought about that. Frank turned to the rest of the team. "There will be growing pains. But we're going to come together. We're going to improve. Now everybody circle around so I can show you the first play."

* * *

At dinner that night, Frank smeared lard onto his bread with a knife and stuffed it into his mouth. His dark mood was palpable and the table was silent except for chewing.

Lydia gently began conversation. "What happened at the plant this week, Frank?"

His mouth full, he replied, "The Rouge is what it is. It doesn't change."

"What about the football squad?"

He swallowed, then blew a frustrated sigh out of his mouth. "Yesterday a player ran the wrong way and scored for the other team."

His three children giggled. The tension was gone.

"Is that funny?" he said.

His eight-year-old nodded. "Yeah."

"Everybody makes mistakes," said Lydia.

Frank's eyes grew large and agitated. "But he did it *three times*!"

Now the children were doubled over, laughing. Frank didn't see the humor at all.

"How is that possible?" asked his daughter, giggling. She was fifteen and sharp.

"He got confused between defense and offense. He thought he was on defense."

"But—" she said.

"I know what you're gonna say, and no the end zone doesn't change. He just gets confused."

"He sounds dumb," said the eight-year-old.

"Dear—" said Lydia.

"She's not wrong," replied Frank.

"Dad, what if you just made him play defense only?" asked the fifteen-year-old. "That way he couldn't make any more mistakes."

"We can't do that. Everybody plays both offense and defense."

"Then maybe you could make two different teams?"

Frank paused. "You're suggesting dividing the squad into separate defensive and offensive platoons?"

His daughter shaped an imaginary mountain of food with her fork. "Some people are better at playing offense and some people are better at playing defense."

Her father thought about it, then shook his head no. "There will never be a two-platoon system. The fans wouldn't stand for it. Lydia, I'll help you wash up. Remember, I need your help in the morning."

* * *

Saturday morning. Frank and Lydia parked their automobile in front of the St. Vincent de Paul salvage bureau on Jefferson Blvd. Through the glass storefront they could see the used goods inside.

"I still don't know why you need me for this," said Lydia.

"You have to help me find the right leather," he said.

"It doesn't really matter what kind of leather."

"You're going to be the one cutting and stapling it. It could be too thick, too thin."

Lydia put her chin into her hand and rested there. She made no movement to exit the automobile. "I don't know why you're pursuing this," she said.

"Because if they play one scrimmage game without anything, it will be a disaster, and then nobody will come back, no matter what I promised them."

After a lengthy pause, she said, "Okay."

He seized her hand and kissed the back of it.

Inside the store, Lydia chortled a greeting. A man polishing a scuffed brown side table peered at her over his spectacles.

"It's Lady Pappas, in the flesh," he said.

"And Mister Pappas," added Frank.

"What can I do for both of you?"

"We're looking for leather," said Lydia.

"The older and the cheaper, the better," Frank added.

The man nodded. "Old and cheap is the name of our game. We've got something over here." He led them to a straight back chair with leather seat and leather back.

Frank sized it up. "I would need sixteen of these, more or less."

"I don't know if we could do that," the man said. "I'd have to call the main office."

"How much would it cost?" said Frank.

"Five dollars."

"For sixteen chairs?"

"No, for one."

Lydia and Frank exchanged alarmed glances. "Thank you for your time," said Frank, "but I have a better idea."

* * *

At the practice field, Frank gathered the players around a stack of yellow felt that he'd carted onto the grass.

He selected a large piece of felt from the stack, then handed it to Luka, who fit his head through the large hole that Lydia had cut in the middle of it the night before. The yellow pad rested on Luka's shoulders and lopped six inches over the edge of each shoulder.

"These, gentlemen, are your shoulder pads." He adjusted the pads and stood back and beamed "It's a perfect fit."

"It's too big, coach," said a voice.

"Nonsense!" Frank said. "And my wife made it, so no complaints."

Carl Bernheimer picked up one of the pads from the pile. "Yellow, coach?"

"It was on discount."

"What happened to leather?" said a player. "I think these should be made of leather."

"Yeah," said another, "I seen a team wearing leather once. On their heads too!"

Frank swung a palm around the circle, as if warning off future criticism. "You oughta be thankful! Truth is, we didn't have this much protection when I played and today there's fellas runnin around in face masks! What'll they think of next?" He shook his head.

Then his eyes landed on Luka. "Come here, you big oaf."

The large Croatian stepped forward. Frank selected two smaller rectangles of felt, then used a knife to cut two lengths of thin rope from a spool. "Tie these around your thighs."

Luka obediently tied the felt pads around his thighs. He looked like a bizarre gladiator prepped poorly for battle.

"This is how you'll dress for the first scrimmage on Saturday," said Frank.

"Against who?"

"A gang of scrubs from Mount Pleasant. No worries, they're terrible too. Now let's go over the plays."

* * *

The day of the first scrimmage, the three black players arrived early to draw chalk lines on the grass. Simmons gathered an armful of rocks to set the lines.

"Coach, what's the distance again?" he said.

"It's every ten yards," Frank said.

Simmons shook his head. "We didn't play nothing like this in Mississippi."

Frank shrugged. "Me neither. We didn't have out-of-bounds either. Here comes another new addition to the game."

A man dressed in a black-and-white vertical striped shirt and a pair of dress slacks arrived on the scene.

"You must be Rosenberg," said Frank.

"You must be Coach Pappas," the man replied.

Frank eyed the new arrival. "You're going to call it fair and square, okay? No putting your thumb on the scale."

"Of course not."

"And you would tell us if the other squad tried to buy you off, correct?"

The man rolled up his sleeves. "I cannot be bought."

One by one, the other players arrived, each carrying the yellow felt pads and their homemade athletic gear. Finally a red bus rolled up to the fairground, a bedsheet reading *Mt Pleasant Bulls* hanging from its open window.

The Ford team watched as their opponents spilled out of the bus. Some men had silver hair; younger ones had paunches. A pair of young women wearing fur stoles and flapper dresses stumbled down the steps, linked arm in arm, giggling and trying to hide their flasks. One player guzzled from a brown glass bottle, burped, and chucked it backwards over his shoulder. Another lay down on the grass and went to sleep.

"This is not a serious team," said Luka.

"Exactly," said Frank.

"We can take them," added Simmons. He clapped his hands. "Come on, y'all, circle up and let's get ready."

* * *

The victory celebration was held later that afternoon at a nineteenth-century pool hall on Mack Avenue. There, eleven grinning members of the football squad passed cold bottles of Faygo soda pop to one another. Clouds of white chalk dust coated hands and drifted in the air. The well-trodden chestnut floorboards shone and squeaked beneath their boots.

"They couldn't run," said one player.

"Their defense had more holes than a block of cheese," said another.

"It was a real surprise," said a third.

Frank returned from the bar bearing three more bottles of soda in each hand. "Here you go, boys. A good takeoff."

"Crème soda is the best," said Bernheimer.

Luka reached for a darker one. "I like rock 'n' rye."

"The scrimmages will get harder," said Frank. He hoisted his bottle into the air. "Gentlemen—to you, to me, to us, and to Henry Ford."

Hesitant clinks to the last item, but the men drank anyways. Then the pool hall manager sidled up to Frank's elbow.

"Pappas, there's three men outside who say they're with you."

"So let them in."

"They're Negroes."

Frank rolled his eyes. "Let them in anyways."

"We don't want that kind of business."

He turned to the proprietor. "Do you own a Ford Motor Company vehicle?"

"Oh yes," the owner replied proudly, "a Model T."

"Those men built that vehicle. They also helped win our first scrimmage today. You can let them in."

Frowning, the manager went outside, then returned with Simmons and the other two blacks from the foundry. The three came over and exchanged quick handshakes with the squad.

"First time I've seen the inside of this place," said Simmons, looking around.

"You play carom billiards?" said Frank.

"No sir."

"Somebody teach these men how to shoot some proper pool," the coach announced, slapping Simmons on the back. The worker grinned.

* * *

Frank's youngest daughter kneeled on a stool in their kitchen, shaping balls of cookie dough and placing them on a baking sheet. Lydia stood at the sink scrubbing another sheet clean. A plate of hot chocolate chip cookies was cooling on the kitchen table.

"Frankie dear, come try one of Evelyn's cookies," she said.

No response.

"Where is your father?"

The daughter looked over. "Daddy's looking out the window."

Lydia walked over and looked. In the living room, her husband was standing on one leg next to the side table, his other leg lifted and perched on the windowsill. He was holding the lace curtain aside while his eyes scanned the street.

"What are you doing?" she said.

Frank shifted his toothpick from one side of his mouth to the other. "Waiting for Jimmy to get home."

"Why don't you just sit outside on the porch and wait?"

He waved off the suggestion. "I need to surprise him this time."

"Evelyn helped make some chocolate chip cookies."

He returned his foot to the floor and grew tense. "There —he just walked by. I'll be back."

Frank bolted out of the house and onto the sidewalk. His heavy footsteps nearly cracked the sidewalk beneath his feet.

"Jimmy," he shouted.

The younger man was already on his own porch, unlacing his shoes. "Say, you've got a lot of nerve, Pappas. I always get thirsty passing your house but it appeared that you weren't home."

"We can have a drink some other time," said Frank, "I have to keep this short. I need a favor, Jimmy."

The assistant athletic director stood up fully and clamped his hands on either side of his waist and cocked his head to the side. "Let's hear it."

"I need to borrow a bucking machine. The one you use for hits."

"We only have two of those."

Frank fought to keep his voice level. "If you want a good squad by November, then I gotta drill 'em right."

"I heard you beat the Mt. Pleasant scrubs."

"We did."

"Straight?"

He grinned. "Mostly."

"How so?"

"I tipped the official fifty cents at halftime. He made a couple good calls."

Jimmy looked at him with disgust. "Our janitors scrape stuff like you off the underside of the bleachers."

"So take me to court. It built their confidence. Half the team barely speaks English and don't know how to play."

"All right," said Jimmy. "When do you want to pick it up?"

"Pick it up? You're gonna deliver it. Send a couple of your college boys in a truck. I need it by Tuesday afternoon at the fairgrounds. Thanks pal."

Frank slapped Jimmy's elbow, winked, then stomped off down the street. "Very cooperative," shouted Jimmy.

* * *

Luka smashed shoulder first into the padded side of the bucking machine. It was an agricultural instrument that had been tinkered with by the university to serve as a tackling dummy. Frank stood inside the contraption, his feet riding the bottom rails, his hands gripping the overhead rails. His weight kept the thing from sliding, mostly.

"Harder!" Frank shouted.

The lineup of players took their turns sprinting into the bucking machine, knocking it back a few inches with every hit.

"One more time!" Frank shouted.

"Why can't we just use a dummy?" said Simmons, rubbing his neck and shoulders.

"They're not heavy enough and even if they were, they don't move. This imitates the sliding of a human."

The players dutifully lined up for another run. When it was Luka's turn, Frank said, "Push into it! Go!"

Luka gritted his teeth and collided with the machine at full sprint.

"It killed your mother!"

Growling, Luka gripped the post with his arms and pushed harder. His thick glutes and muscular thighs drove the entire bucking machine three yards back.

"Whoa, whoa," shouted Frank.

Luka pulled himself off the post, and Frank stepped out from the machine. Two rows of freshly-plowed dirt had been dug in the green clover.

"Shitballs, you're strong," he muttered.

"Did I do good?" said Luka, hands on head, gasping for breath.

Frank slapped him on the back. "Not too bad, ya lunk."

Then he turned to the group and drew an imaginary line on the ground with the side of his hand. "Line up here and let's do some running. Twenty yards and stop. Repeated five times, then rest. Hop to it, boys."

Frank watched the men sprinting and stopping and sprinting. His clenched hand relaxed, and the tiniest glimmer of a smile appeared at the corner of his mouth.

* * *

Two weeks later, Frank stood forlornly on the sidelines of the next scrimmage match, his hands balled into tight fists once again.

On field, Luka hiked the pigskin to Greniak, who fell back and looked for an open man. Two runners were covered left and right, so he tucked the ball under his arm and tried to run it himself. On his third step, an opposing lineman broke free of the scrum and plowed into him with forearms. Greniak hit the ground like a sack of cement dropped off a roof.

"Get up!" shouted Frank.

The back shook the cobwebs out of his head and tried to stand up, then fell down again. His teammates helped him to his feet a second time

Frank glanced over at the chalkboard. They'd paid a neighborhood kid five cents to keep score. It read *Ford 6, Albion 59.*

"Three more minutes, boys," Frank said. He blew air out of his mouth and glanced at his wristwatch.

When the game was finally put out of its misery, the men limped off the field.

* * *

Sunday dinner, and Lydia placed the dish of lamb chops in the center of the table. It was covered in a green fuzz of Greek spices. The scent of garlic and herbs filled the room.

"It's quite hot everybody," she warned. "Sweetie, do you want to serve the table?"

Frank slumped in his chair. Purple pouches of sadness hung from his eyes. His shoulders had collapsed upon his frame like a building whose foundation had shifted.

"Frank?"

His eyes flicked up to his wife. "Yeah, sorry."

He summoned up enough energy to pick up the knife and serving fork. He softly speared the chops, one by one, and laid them on the plates that his children offered. Then he took the large serving spoon and ladled the fragrant oil across each one.

"The famous Pappas family recipe," he said, "enjoy."

He sat back in his chair. Lydia took the utensils and set a lamb chop on his plate. He stared at it. He poked the meat with his fork. Then he looked up at the ceiling, arms crossed, his mind somewhere else.

Lydia took her seat and served herself. "So how did the team do?"

He muttered something unintelligible. The meaning was clear.

"Well, I hope they perform better next time."

"It was another scrub team," he said. "They were called Wheat Fields AC. They were supposed to play just decent. Instead they beat us like a gong."

"So maybe you should take a break."

"Well, Tuesday practice is cancelled for rain anyways."

"I mean, maybe you should take a break until spring."

This suggestion brought her husband back to life. "Impossible. I have to show those college boys that Ford boys are tougher. The game is next month and we can't miss it."

"Don't you think that the world already knows about you? Henry Ford's name is everywhere. Everybody is buying those Model Ts."

"Yeah dad," said the fifteen-year-old, "everybody knows about Detroit."

This got Frank steaming mad. "It's not that. Listen, I work with college boys after they're all grown up. They sit in their nice offices and big oak desks and think they're better than we are. Telling us what to do, every day. I'm fed up. They've never had to really work, not like us downstairs on the line. And I wanna beat 'em."

He grabbed his silverware and began sawing at his lamb and stuffing it into his mouth. Lydia watched her husband and smiled to herself.

* * *

On a bright Saturday afternoon, Frank and his squad sat on a portion of wooden bleachers, wearing their workmen's blue denim and dark overcoats. Around them were hundreds of young college students in wool sweaters, their shiny cheeks reddened with cold and enthusiasm. Nearby a set of trumpets, fifes, and bass drums beat out a simple martial song.

On field, the University of Detroit team wore matching red-and-white striped turtleneck sweaters with high-hipped brown padded breeches. Their opponents, the DePaul Blue Demons, were taking a drubbing.

"Look at that!" said Frank, pointing at the player marked number 14. He was sprinting down the field, knees pumping high, right arm held out to ward off attackers. He arrived in the end zone, his arms lifted overhead.

"Ooooh he's fast," said Simmons.

"Nineteen years old," someone said.

"Who we got that can mark him?"

"Bernheimer's fast," someone said.

Carl Bernheimer pulled his hat nervously over his face. "Naw, I can't mark him."

The kicker cleared the field goal, and the scoreboard flipped to *Titans 28, Visitors 13.*

"Well," said Frank, "if we can't match their speed, we'll rely on our other strengths."

"What's that?"

"We're tough sons of bitches."

"Are we?" said someone.

Frank turned at the squad and glared. "Yeah."

"Plus we got Luka," said Bernheimer.

The large Croat was watching the game, mouth open. Greniak tossed popcorn into it, which startled him.

"He never saw no football game before," whispered Simmons to the coach.

"No worries," replied Frank quietly. "Linemen block and rush. He'll figure it out."

"Say, coach," said Simmons, "I been meaning to say, you got me running, but I really want to throw the ball. I mean, I throw better than Greniak."

"I know you do," said Frank.

"So—"

"The answer is still no."

Simmons opened his mouth as if to say something, then closed it.

A man came up the aisle selling cold ginger ale from a tray that hung from around his neck. Frank motioned to him and asked for ten bottles and handed the man a dollar. They were passed around the group.

"Our squad has a strong future," said Frank. Then he pointed at the field. "DePaul plays well too. They should be playing good football for a long time."

At halftime, the band took to the field and provided backup for the male cheerleaders, who used bullhorns made of aluminum sheeting to lead the crowd in chants. The spectators clapped in time and answered the questions.

Then a pair of female cheerleaders joined them, swishing their skirts. On cue, the male cheerleaders picked them up by the waists and spun them around in circles, their feet pointing at the sky, their thighs flashing in the sun.

The auto workers nudged one another and grinned.

Frank ignored the titillation and scanned the crowd for familiar faces. That's when he noticed Jimmy, who'd just arrived at the scene. He caught the assistant athletic director's eye, and they nodded at one another. Next to Jimmy was an older gentleman in a suit and Borsalino fedora. He carried himself with gravity.

Talk now? mouthed Frank.

Jimmy shook his head no, then thumbed towards the serious man next to him.

The serious man noticed Jimmy's communication and swiveled around. He took note of Frank and the auto workers sitting behind him.

Who's that? the man mouthed.

Frank watched as Jimmy pointed to the squad, spoke rapidly, and gestured from them to the field. It was clear he was explaining the upcoming game.

The man peered at Frank and the ragtag auto worker squad. Suddenly his face darkened and his brow creased in disapproval.

Frank kept an eye on him until the man left.

* * *

The Müllerhaus was a venerable German restaurant in Hamtramck, and tonight the supper crowd was chattering when Frank entered. Standing inside the front door, he spotted Jimmy at a table near the back. He stomped across the restaurant, holding his hat against his belly, giving wide berth to the waiters carrying trays of schnitzel and sausage.

Jimmy stood up as he approached and offered his hand. "Frank, thanks for coming. I'd like you to meet John McGregor, the athletic director."

Another man was at the table, square-jawed and handsome in an older way, and he stood halfway up from his chair and pumped Frank's hand twice with surprising strength. "Pleasure, Mister Pappas. Jimmy's told me a lot of things about you."

"They're all true," said Frank, taking his seat, "even the bad ones. What's new at the university?"

McGregor thought about it. "Some people want raise funds to build a tower commemorating the young soldiers the university lost in the war."

Frank nodded. "I'll contribute. May it never happen again."

"Indeed."

The waiter arrived and took their order. When he'd left, Jimmy said, "How is the training going?"

"To be honest, about what I expected," replied Frank. "They've memorized all the plays. We're conditioning best we can. A few more scrimmages should tighten them up. A few might even have proper footwear soon."

He grinned, but Jimmy and McGregor didn't reciprocate. "That's the reason we wanted to see you, Frank," said Jimmy.

Frank's ears pricked up in alarm. "The footwear?"

Jimmy shook his head. "Mister McGregor would like to explain."

"No," said the athletic director, "I think you should explain, Jimmy."

The young man grew uncomfortable. "Frank, it was brought to our attention that your squad is carrying three Negroes."

Frank realized that this wasn't going to be a friendly dinner. "Yes," he said.

A rueful expression appeared on Jimmy's face. "Our college players won't take the field against any squad with Negroes."

"It's only three out of sixteen, Jimmy. We already talked about this."

Jimmy held up a warning finger. "We're also getting some pushback from high up."

Frank turned to the boss. "John, is there a policy against playing Negroes?"

"No," the athletic director said.

"So somebody just decided to spy on our practices," he said. "Is that right?"

"No, not exactly—"

Frank suddenly understood. He looked back at Jimmy. "Was it that man I saw you with on Saturday? At the game?"

His neighbor looked uncomfortable. "I can't say one way or—"

"Who was he?"

"A member of the board of trustees.," said McGregor.

"And he didn't like the composition of our squad."

"Frank—" said Jimmy.

"Did you put it to a vote with the players themselves?"

Jimmy grew impatient. "As a matter of fact, I did, Frank. And they voted not to play against any Negroes."

Frank sighed. "I've bent over backwards to build this squad, just because you asked—"

"Mister Pappas," interrupted McGregor, "you understand that we appreciate everything you've done to form this squad, but if you can't do it according to our wishes, then we simply can't have a game."

The waiter brought their meals. McGregor examined his sauerbraten. "My grandmother wouldn't recognize this. They're changing the recipes."

"Things change, McGregor," Frank said. "We all might as well get used to it."

* * *

The basement speakeasy was dark and crowded, and Frank's eyes were slow to adjust to the dimness. A thick blanket of tobacco smoke and sweet whiskey fumes hung in the air. The entry to this blind pig was through a false cellar door on the rear of a boarding house.

At least thirty people crammed in here, mostly men, a few off-duty cops. They were playing cards, gambling, laughing. Bare electric lamps hung on each wall.

Frank squinted and scanned the room. There. At a table near to the sideboard that passed for a bar sat five nervous white men.

It was the group from the foundry.

Frank grabbed a nearby chair, lifted it in the air over his head, and carried it to their table. Then he brought it down so hard on the floor so hard that the wooden boards kicked up.

The men jumped in their seats, startled. Frank spun the chair so that the back was facing the table and sat down across it with his legs spread wide. He drummed his fingers on the back of the chair while he looked all five in the eyes.

"Whiskey," he said.

One of the men motioned to the bartender. A small glass of rye appeared in front of him.

"You all know me by a variety of different nasty words," he said, "but my name is Mister Pappas. That is how you will address me. Now say my name."

"Mister Pappas," the men said.

He nodded. "Good. You boys all still like to fight?"

Hesitation. They looked around at one another, unsure how to respond.

"You all better say yes," Frank said.

"Yes," said the five men.

"Okay, I've got an assignment for you. If you do it right, I take you off probation and you come back to work. If you do it wrong, you never work at Ford Motor Company again."

"What do we gotta do?" said one. He was thin with predatory eyes and a sharp nose.

Frank pulled a small notebook and pencil from the pocket of his coat and placed them in the middle of the table. "I sure hope one of you knows how to write, because somebody needs to take some notes."

* * *

Sunset, late October. On the practice field, the university football team finished their last play for the day. Their coach blew his whistle and shouted for the players to get to the locker room and clean up.

A short distance away, on McNichols Ave, the thin man with the sharp nose from the foundry loitered. He had a lit cigarette and leaned against a telephone pole lazily enjoying it, appearing to wait for a streetcar.

A quarter hour later, a group of four college players emerged from the locker room in the fieldhouse. The man flicked his cigarette butt onto the ground and quietly ran to catch up to the young men.

Staying several yards behind, he followed them eastward down Grove Street and then followed them as they turned right on Linwood. By now, the sun had disappeared behind the houses, cloaking the street in darkness, and the boys' wet hair had begun to freeze against their scalps.

Halfway down the block, before they could reach Puritan Avenue, the thin man suddenly shouted at them.

"You there! Young men!"

The four college boys turned.

"Can we help you?" one of the boys shouted back.

"Yeah, I'm a bit lost, and I was hoping you can point me in the right direction."

"Where are you looking to go?"

The foundry worker approached them and pulled a knife from his pocket. "To a football game."

At that, the other four white men from the foundry stepped out from the darkness. They'd positioned themselves in bushes, behind trees, and in dark driveways. All four wielded baseball bats. They circled the group in a matter of seconds.

It was an ambush.

The four college players quickly arranged themselves back-to-back. "Hey what's this about?" said one.

The thin man joined them, and now the five foundry workers advanced in a tightening circle. "It's about your attitude towards the Negroes," said one.

The players didn't understand this. "You tough guys are coming at us because of our attitude towards Negroes?" said one.

"Yeah," replied a foundry worker, "we think you ought to play football with them."

The college boys looked at one another, confused. "Why didn't the Negroes themselves come out?" said the spokesman.

"That's not your business, boys," said another foundry worker.

One of the players tried to make a break for it. The men from the foundry were ready. The player quickly found a Louisville slugger in his belly and dropped to the ground.

At that, the brawl began in earnest. It didn't last long. In a short time all four college players were on the ground. The foundry workers stood over them, kicking them with their boots, hitting them with the bats.

The thin man with the sharp eyes lit another cigarette and watched. "Keep it gentle," he said to the others, "nothing too rough. Just a few love taps."

Eventually he went over and held out an arm and broke it up. The other foundry workers pulled away from the college boys.

The leader looked down at the bloodied players. "So what did you learn here tonight?"

"We're gonna play the Negroes," muttered one. Another spit out a tooth. A third was quietly crying.

"That's right. Thank you for your time, gentlemen." He flicked his cigarette onto the players.

A minute later, the foundry workers vanished into the

darkness, leaving the four college boys bloodied and bruised and moaning in the mud.

* * *

Frank sat on his porch, his ceramic mug in hand. His youngest child was playing with a spare tire on the small square of grass.

Jimmy stepped out of his house and walked over. His customary saunter looked more subdued than usual.

"Evening, Frank," he said.

"Evening, Jimmy," he replied.

"You remember the complaint that Mister McGregor and I outlined for you the other night."

Frank sipped from his mug. "I do indeed. About the Negroes on my squad."

"Yes—the players on our team have informed us that they have changed their minds. They no longer have an objection to playing your squad as scheduled."

Frank looked shocked. "Is that so? What caused this change of heart?"

"It seems a few got roughed up pretty bad by a group of fellas who, um, demanded that they change their attitude towards Negroes."

"My goodness," said Frank, "curbside court really has changed, hasn't it?"

"It seems."

"Certainly the Negroes are growing more aggressive in their demands."

"These were white men."

Frank burst out in a loud chortle. "I'll be a monkey's uncle! This world is truly a strange place." He shook his head at the marvel of it all.

Jimmy ran a hand through the back of his hair. "After consulting with the trustees, the director has decided to reinstate the game. It will take place on November fifteenth, the Saturday before Thanksgiving, as planned."

"That is excellent news," said Frank, "and quite a surprise."

"I bet," said Jimmy curtly.

He walked back to his house without a word. Frank lifted his ceramic mug to his face and grinned.

* * *

The next day, Frank arrived at the Rouge full of vim and vigor. He ran workflow meetings with his subordinates, attended efficiency meetings with finance department, and avoided meetings with rumored labor organizers. He also signed off on end-of-probation papers for five workers in the foundry.

At two in the afternoon, he sank back into his chair in his tiny office and locked his hands at the back of his head and kicked his feet up on his desk. He closed his eyes. A small snore escaped his meaty lips.

A sharp rap at the door, and his eyes flew open.

"What?" he shouted.

"Mister Pappas," said a female voice.

He pulled his feet off his desk and leaned over and yanked open the door. It was a secretary from the executive suite. She wore a pencil skirt and a bit too much red lipstick and carried a wolf's glint in her eye.

"This better be good, Alice," he said.

"Mister Weber wants to see you," she replied.

He rolled his eyes. "Tell him it can wait."

"He said you would say that, and he told me to tell you that it's about your football squad."

Frank paused. He hadn't known that word about his extracurricular activity had made its way up to the top brass.

"I'll be over shortly," he grumbled.

* * *

It was a quarter-mile walk to the executive office building, and Frank felt like he was headed to the gallows. This was a conditioned response. The fellows in the big offices rarely called him for anything other than a dressing down.

He entered the executive building through the heavy iron door, nodded at the guards, headed down the hall to the fourth door on the right. He entered a small anteroom.

At a table, Alice was typing rapidly on a Hammond type-writer. She wore a set of earphones whose cord ran to a dicta-phone machine that rested on a tiny secretarial desk next to her.

"I'm here," he said.

She didn't reply, engrossed in her typing. Frank crept around her desk and clapped his hands three times next to her ear.

Startled, her body jerked violently, and the earphones flew off her head. "Applesauce!" she said.

"You're too old to say that," he replied.

"What a piece of work you are, Frank."

"Can I go in?"

"Maybe in a minute," she replied.

Alice stood up and disappeared into the adjacent office. She came back and nodded. "Be careful of the mood."

"You or him?" said Frank.

"Now both."

He blew a kiss at her, then went into the executive's office. William Weber was sitting in his swivel leather chair, his long legs perched on his oak desk. He wore the customary gray double-breasted suit, all four buttons closed tightly. A pair of shiny brogues on his feet cost more than a worker's monthly salary and his hair was slicked back. In his hands was a paper report.

"Pappas, you're not going to believe this," he said.

Frank sat down in the small chair opposite him. "What's that?"

"Three years ago, King Henry acquires the bankrupt Lincoln Motors, a luxury automotive brand that produces automobiles that no Ford customer can afford. Hank spends millions to relocate and upgrade their operations. We force out their founders. We project a five-year-long bloodbath on our balance sheets. Marketing tells us to stop crying and recognize that consumers want to"—he made finger quotes —"aspire to something they can't afford. None of it adds up."

"I said it was a terrible idea," said Frank.

"And now look."

Weber threw the report on the table.

Frank waited for a reply. "What is it?"

"People can't buy Lincolns fast enough! I mean, the division is *profitable*. Even the goddamned president of the United States is riding around in one. It makes no sense."

"I'm no businessman, sir, but sometimes it's good to be wrong," said Frank. "I'm on the weekly purchase plan myself."

Weber shook his head. "I disagree with that entire philosophy. We're training the consumers to save for a car they can't afford. What's next? Soon we'll be acting like a bank and lending the suckers money to buy the damned things."

Frank sucked on a tooth. "That seems dangerous."

Weber stood up. "Such speculation will bring down this nation. We're in for a big crash. Mark my words."

"Eh," said Frank, "I'll believe it when I see it."

The executive barked a derisive laugh and parked himself on the edge of his desk. "Meanwhile, you wouldn't believe some of the nutty ideas floating around this floor. Did you hear about Fordlandia?"

"The thing in Brazil?"

Weber nodded. "King Henry is annoyed by the British monopoly over rubber, so he plans to buy four thousand square miles of rubber trees in Brazil and populate it with ten thousand local workers. He also plans to administer the whole project from the fourth floor of this very building." His eyeballs rolled around in his skull. "Pshaw."

Frank checked his wristwatch. "So why did you want to see me, Mister Weber?"

That jerked Weber back to the summons. "Ah, yes—I've been informed that you've formed a football squad with a few of the men on the factory floor." He looked amused.

"How did you hear that?"

The executive ignored the question. "So, here's the issue. My neighbor has a son who plays on the University of Detroit varsity squad. Word got out about some kind of a beating that a few of the boys encountered the other night. Now the parents are terrified that the students are being targeted."

"That is not true," said Frank.

"Do you know something about that?"

"No," said Frank, "but I wish that it never would've happened, and I'm sure it won't happen again."

William looked at him warily. "The game is scheduled for November, correct?"

Frank nodded. "The fifteenth, one week before Thanksgiving."

"And there won't be any problems?"

"Of what kind?"

"Violence."

"I don't understand."

William gave him a skeptical look. "I could shut this whole thing down if you don't say the right things, Pappas."

Frank drew a deep breath and leaned forward. "The game has changed, Mister Weber. Back when I played, the game used to be open meadows, no lines, no pads. We elbowed any poor sap in the face who was stupid enough to get in the way of our flying wedge. That's all different now. There are rules and officials and strategy. It's no donnybrook, not anymore."

The executive leaned back and stroked his chin. "Keep talking. I'm almost persuaded."

"Furthermore, this game will be good for city spirit. It'll bring the classes together."

Weber raised an eyebrow. "I never took you for a socialist, Pappas."

"Oh, I'm no socialist. But you and I are from different classes, sir, and we've always got on well."

"True."

"That's all I'm saying. We should want more of that. Plus, this city needs a crosstown rivalry. Every city has one. It's good for civic spirit."

"Town and gown," said Weber, musing.

"It could even be an annual match."

The executive nodded. "All right, I'm sold. You may proceed."

"Thank you, sir."

"What does the squad need to play?"

Frank answered quickly. "Uniforms, sir. And cleats and pads."

"Uniforms will be easy. I'll get the eight-fingered boys in upholstery to make some quality uniforms. The other things, arrange with a shop in the city and route the invoice through my office."

Frank couldn't hide the excitement in his voice. "Thank you very much, Mister Weber. We're tough on the floor and we intend to be even tougher on the field."

"My pleasure. Say, we can even put up Ford recruitment tents on the day, maybe have a small fair. It's an easy way to advertise. Everybody wins."

"Sounds great." Frank stood up, shook the executive's hand, and headed for the door.

"Pappas," said the executive, "two more things."

In the doorway, Frank stopped. "Yes, Mister Weber."

"Whatever skull-cracking monkey business you arranged to intimidate those college boys, knock it off. That type of behavior exists on the other side of the line of civility. It won't be crossed at Ford Motor Company."

Frank swallowed nervously. "Yes sir, it won't happen again."

"And no more talk about social classes."

"Yes sir."

The executive kept an eye on the foreman as the door closed behind him.

* * *

The next week, the squad played an away scrimmage game. Using a borrowed bus, Frank picked up the players from the fairgrounds and pointed the vehicle westward down Grand River Avenue. Soon the smooth pavement turned to mud, and the bus rutted and jounced for two hours.

"Where we goin again, coach?" shouted a player.

At the wheel, Frank downshifted and spun the wheel to avoid a large patch of wet mud in the road. Then switched his cigarette from one side of his mouth to the other. "Brighton."

"Who's this team?"

"The BK Avengers," Bernheimer said.

"I don't know much about them," said Frank, "but we're gonna play and then get out before dark. It's a long drive each way."

Finally the bus rolled into an open recreation area and the squad poured out. The field was a perfect rectangle, one hundred yards by forty yards, marked with white chalk on the green grass. A group of thirty spectators had assembled on three rows of neat wooden bleachers. A vendor sold sandwiches and hot coffee from a folding table. A white banner stretched between two poles read *BK Avengers Conquer All.*

"Is beautiful," said Luka.

"Not to us," said Simmons, scanning the crowd.

The players donned their new black Ford uniforms. Some began pregame stretches on the sidelines—hip stretches, toe touches, lunges. Others laced up their new pads inside their breeches.

Greniak limped over to Frank holding his head. "Coach, I don't feel so good."

"You took a bad hit last game," Frank said.

"I don't feel like I can throw the ball today."

Sighing, Frank scanned the crowd. "Can you give us at least one half?"

"I can try."

"Thanks buddy," he said.

The squad huddled up for the pregame meeting. Reading from his clipboard, Frank gave them a few pointers, reminded them of their strengths and weaknesses, and then read off the starting lineup. The squad put their hands into the middle.

"Who are we?" said Frank.

"Rouge!" they shouted in unison.

They took the field. Standing beside Frank were the substitutes. Today, those included three black players. They were consulting one another.

"Why you keepin us out today, coach?" said Simmons. "We always play."

"Don't bother me right now," Frank replied.

"But—"

"It's not personal."

Simmons exchanged glances with the other two black players.

The match started and Frank studied the opponents. The BK Avengers were mostly corn-fed farm boys, early twenties at most. He analyzed their playing. Some could run, some could block, some knew the game. There were no obvious flaws.

Bernheimer stood at his elbow. "This squad don't play like city squads do."

"Yeah," said Frank, "nobody's fighting a hangover out here."

Bernheimer looked at the parking area, his hand shading his eyes from the afternoon sun. "Why are the cars all painted?"

Frank turned around. The lot was full of Model Ts, black as usual, but the hoods had been painted white.

"I don't know," he said.

On the field, Simmons took the ball from Luka, then made a half-hearted toss to a runner. It fell short.

"Dammit, that's the third one," said someone.

Greniak walked slowly over to the sidelines. "I can't do it," he said.

Frank shook his head no. "Come on, man, just give us a few more plays—"

The Polish back suddenly buckled at the knees and fell down onto the ground. Two members of the squad rushed over and attended to him. They helped him sit up. Someone lifted a canteen to his mouth.

"He just needs a minute," said Frank.

"Coach—" said Simmons.

"Not now!" snapped Frank.

"Put Simmons in," said Bernheimer.

The coach crossed his arms. "No, it's not going to happen."

By now, the squad had gathered on the sidelines. The BK Avengers were standing in the middle of the field, waiting.

"Men, somebody has to throw the ball," said Frank. "It's not hard. You fall back a quarter of the way between the halfback and full back. You catch the ball from Luka and then throw it to the runner who is assigned to catch it. It's a simple task. Nobody wants to do it?"

He waited for a volunteer. Nobody spoke.

"Make it Simmons," said Luka.

Frank looked at him aghast. "You don't speak all season, and now you pipe up? Really?"

"Coach Pappas, we don't want to play unless Simmons throws the ball," said another.

The squad nodded. Even Greniak said, "It has to be him."

Frank rubbed his forehead. "Simmons, come here."

He walked a few yards away from the group. Simmons followed him, clapping his hands, anxious to get on the field.

"Coach—"

Frank cut him off. "Now you listen up. I want to tell you three things. One, don't run the ball yourself, not against this squad. Two, do not respond to anybody on the other team. Three, stick close to Luka. Understand?"

The black player looked at his coach. "I understand."

"I knew you would," Frank replied. "If you want to know why, take a look at our hosts right now."

Simmons looked up. All the players, spectators, coaches, and officials were watching their conversation. Most had crossed their arms and wore angry faces.

"You grew up in Mississippi, right? You remember this feeling?"

"Aw shit," said Simmons, "this is a sundown town."

"Not officially, but yes."

"Why didn't you tell us?"

"Because you wouldn't have come. And then I couldn't keep my promise to get you out of the foundry. You understand my dilemma?"

Simmons frowned. "Yeah, coach."

"Now get out there and throw the ball safely. When the game ends, we will form a protective ring around you and the two other Negroes and escort you directly to the bus."

"All right."

"And Simmons, there's a fourth thing."

"What?"

Frank lowered his voice to a whisper. "We have to lose."

"Come again?"

"We can't beat this team. As soon as you set foot on this field, they have to win. Understand?"

"Yeah." Simmons bit his lip in frustration, then drove a fist into his palm.

The squad returned to the game. When Simmons stepped onto the field, the spectators began to boo. The official in his black-and-white striped shirt blew his whistle. He approached Frank.

"He isn't permitted to compete," he said.

"We don't have anyone else who can throw the ball," replied Frank.

"Then you'll have to forfeit."

"Do you want to disappoint all these people?" He gestured to the spectators. "They want to see a game. And all the players want to play one."

The official scratched the side of his neck with an uncomfortable finger. "You're putting us in a difficult position."

"I can make it easier. Let me show you the plan."

Frank lifted his clipboard and pointed to the five-dollar bill that was clipped to it. "Pretty good plan, yeah?"

At first, the official betrayed nothing. "You city people," he finally spat. Then he palmed the bill, turned away, and blew his whistle, signaling the beginning of play.

Frank stayed silent for the remainder of the game. Simmons threw short, direct passes that connected with the runners. Bernheimer scored two touchdowns. The spectators booed constantly, one even throwing a banana on the field.

"Oh no," said Bernheimer. He caught Simmons by the elbow. "Look."

On the sidelines, three men in white robes had arrived. One held a staff with a white flag that read *BK Avengers*.

"What is it mean?" said Luka.

"It means you protect Simmons," said Bernheimer.

Distracted, they started the next play. A lineman got past Luka and flattened Simmons on the ground with a full-force palm to the face. Simmons stood up, woozy. Next, he began throwing the ball out of bounds and forgetting to mark his man on defense. Soon the BK Avengers scored three touchdowns and regained the lead.

When the official blew his whistle at five pm, the other players circled Simmons and ran directly to the bus and climbed aboard and pulled the door shut behind them. Frank was already at the wheel, engine running, and the others had preloaded the gear.

Twenty of the Brighton spectators surrounded the bus, pounding on its sides with their fists. It was a horrible symphony of hate. A bottle flew through the open window and shattered against the interior, showering Bernheimer with shards of glass.

"Off we go!" shouted Frank.

He shifted into first gear, and the vehicle lurched forward. The symphony of fists ended, though some of the spectators followed on foot as long as they could, until the bus accelerated down the road. A police officer waited at the first intersection, his face a rictus of anger, and motioned for the bus to pull over.

Frank drove the vehicle straight past him.

Three minutes later, the town of Brighton receded to nothing in the rearview mirror. "We're safe," said Frank.

At last the squad exhaled. They passed around canteens of water and a bag of navel oranges. The black players sank back into their seats, relieved. Simmons laid a white towel over his face and made a sign of the cross on his chest.

"You all did well," said Frank, at the wheel. "You all showed 'em just how tough Ford boys are."

Simmons yanked the towel off his face. "Somebody shoulda told us what the K stood for, coach."

"I'm not leaving the city again," someone said.

"It's toughened you up," said Frank. "I think you're ready for the university game next weekend."

* * *

On the morning of the final game, Frank sat at the top of the university's bleachers, reflecting on his own athletic past.

As a young man, he'd played on trashy terrain with few or no marked boundaries, against teams made up mostly of thugs. The line between sport and violence had only been drawn recently.

He rolled some tobacco in a paper on his thigh to form a cigarette. He lit it and took one drag, then found himself doubled over, beating his sternum with a fist, a thin line of drool swinging from his mouth like a fishing wire.

He sat up, his breath coming in spurts like a dying beached whale.

"Put down that cigarette, sir," said a voice.

It was Jimmy. He'd come onto the bleachers. Frank watched him hop up onto the boards and lightly run over.

"Or at least let me finish it," Jimmy said.

Frank muttered something unintelligible.

Jimmy sat down next to him. "It's a perfect day for the game, thank Zeus. Cold but sunny. The best you can hope for from November."

"It's not too bad," said Frank.

They sat there, their plumes of breath forming elaborate dragons in the frosty morning air.

"I thank you," the younger man said, "for everything you did this season."

Frank waved his hand in a say-no-more gesture.

"I'm serious, Pappas."

Frank looked at him. "You know how you hooked me, Jimmy? You said we weren't tough at the Rouge."

"I didn't say that," replied Jimmy, "but I implied it."

"Yeah, well—that one comment is what did it."

"No autopsy, no foul."

"I told you, that's still an exaggeration."

"The game really is better now, Pappas."

"Don't I know it. Look at this." Frank gestured to the neatly trimmed grass, the ten-yard markers, the officials tidying up the sidelines. "It's a real sport, by God."

"There's a new team in Chicago that people are saying good things about."

"That so?"

"They call themselves the Bears. They're supposed to play some scrubs here next month. Rumor has it they sold ten thousand tickets on the East Coast."

Frank wrinkled his nose. "Probably a flash in the pan. It's a miracle that packing businessman up in Green Bay didn't lose his franchise, hiring college players the way he did. He approached a couple of our boys."

They both fell silent.

"So who's gonna win today?" said Jimmy.

"I don't care," came the reply.

"Yeah, you do."

"No, Jimmy," said Frank, "I pretend like I care, but really I just want to push people around. I like telling scared chumps what to do." He grinned. "It's the only good thing about getting older. You learn to be honest with yourself."

"You're a fighter."

Frank made a fifty-fifty gesture. "Those days are behind me. I prefer to let others knock around." He coughed once again.

A loud clang echoed from the parking lot behind them. They twisted around and saw the Ford trucks setting up the adjacent fair—the popcorn stands, the ring-toss games, a pony ride, a small Ferris wheel.

"I like these boys on the squad," said Frank. "They work hard at the plant and they work hard on this squad. So we'll just get out there today and do the job and don't take no guff from nobody."

Jimmy cleared his throat. "Our squad has been preparing itself for this match."

"We're ready."

"Promise you won't get hot under the collar."

Frank's mouth rearranged itself into a sad semi-circle. "No, I won't. But the squad is a different story."

* * *

Almost a thousand spectators had filled the stands by two pm. On the sidelines, the Ford squad was warming up their bodies in the chilly air.

Luka waved to his wife and small child in the bleachers. They were both wrapped in heavy gray coats. She lifted the child's arm and waved it back.

"You got a nice little family," Greniak said.

"Thank you, you too," replied Luka.

Greniak looked at him. "I don't have a family."

"Very nice," said Luka, "thank you."

Simmons came around and put an arm across Greniak and steered him away. "Buddy, if you want to change your mind, you just let me know."

"I've decided," Greniak said. "It's too many people watching. You throw better than me anyways."

"All right. You gonna run?"

"Oh yes. And you gonna hit me with one of those long-range bombs."

"I got you."

They slapped hands.

"Gather round," said Frank. The squad circled around him. "This match is the reason I was asked to assemble this squad. The University of Detroit varsity football team, our opponents, are on average twenty years old, unlike most of you." He paused to let that sink in. "Unlike you, they also don't work day jobs. So consider this your final reminder— do *not* allow those runners to get past you, or we'll never show our faces in this city again. Bernheimer, you'll mark their guy Kipling, number fourteen, the one we talked about. Stick with him like glue."

Bernheimer saluted him. "Worst day of my life."

Frank ignored him. "Our only real advantage is we're bigger. Luka can overpower anybody on the line, I'm positive of that. So Luka, you sack the thrower. Drive him backwards as far as you can, then put his spine in the dirt."

Luka gave a thumbs up. "Thank you," he said.

"Everybody, ignore the crowd. It doesn't matter what they shout. Say 'yes, coach' if you understand me."

"Yes coach," shouted the players.

"It's a friendly game, but it's possible these boys view it differently. So keep your cool no matter what. You represent the Ford Motor Company. Now, hands in."

The squad reached in.

"On three," he said. "One, two—"

"Rouge!" they shouted.

The man on the loudspeaker announced *River Rouge foreman Frank Pappas* as the visiting team's coach, and Frank walked to the center of the field, where Jimmy waited for him. Standing alongside him were John MacGregor and William Weber. All four men exchanged handshakes, then turned to pose for the photographer, who was standing with his camera under draped black cloth.

"Looking forward to a good clean game this afternoon, Pappas," said MacGregor, a smile plastered on his face.

"You'll get a game," answered Frank, smiling, "but whether it's clean depends on your boys."

In front of the stands, a group of male cheerleaders shouted chants through large cones of aluminum sheeting. In the stands, the spectators lazily threw popcorn into their mouths and guzzled bottles of ginger ales.

Nearby, the trumpets, fifes, and bass drums began their military march, and the university team burst onto the field wearing their red-and-white striped turtleneck sweaters with brown padded breeches.

The Ford squad took the field a minute later. Greniak represented the squad at center field for the coin toss. The official flipped the coin. It came down heads.

The captains shook hands. The squads faced one another. The official blew the whistle, and the university team kicked the ball high in the air.

The game began, but it didn't last long.

* * *

A day later, Frank woke up, disoriented.

He was stretched out like a corpse, arms crossed over his

chest, in a thin bed in an unfamiliar sterile room. On his body he wore a loose-backed gown of coarse, light-green cotton. He turned his head. Next to his pillow, a tall copper tank thrummed loud and steady. A hose led from the top of the tank to a heavy mask with a leather strap. It hung loosely off the railing of his bed, within arm's reach.

"You're in hospital," said a voice.

Frank looked to the other side of the bed. It was Jimmy, sitting in a chair, one leg crossed over the other. He was smoking a cigarette.

"Henry Ford Hospital," he added.

"What happened?" Frank said.

"You don't remember?"

Frank shook his head. "I remember it was second half ... one of your university boys got caught with a razor blade on the field ... somebody threw a punch—"

"Luka."

"Luka threw a punch, then one of yours jumped on him—"

"And then?"

"I don't remember."

Jimmy stood up and paced. "It was a bench-clearing brawl."

"Oh Christ."

"I'm pretty sure Jesus wasn't there, or he would've stopped it."

"But why am I here? In hospital?"

"Because you got involved. You were swinging hard, smack dab in the middle of it."

"That really doesn't sound like me."

"A thousand people saw it, Pappas. Quite a few leapt onto the field and participated. Then you had a heart attack."

Frank sank back into the pillows and shut his eyes. "God. That's how my papa passed. Where's Lydia?"

"She's outside. I can bring her in."

He lifted a hand. "Wait. How did we end the game?"

"It didn't end, it was abandoned." Jimmy paused. "We tied, if it's still important to you."

Frank grinned. "The boys did good." He looked at Jimmy. "Your boys are cheating pieces of shit."

Jimmy grew visibly upset. "There will be disciplinary action taken."

Frank tried to laugh. It came out like a short, horrible bark. "All this time, Jimmy, we thought it would be the factory boys who would play tough. But here it was the university boys."

"I guess we were wrong," said Jimmy. "The game hasn't changed."

Frank's eyes drifted to the ceiling. "I can't die here."

"The doctors said you should be discharged tomorrow. They expect you to make a full recovery."

"Okay." Frank sighed. "You can bring Lydia in now."

"All right, Frank. Get better."

"Hey Jimmy."

"Yeah."

"We won't do this again next year."

Jimmy gave a rueful grin. "No, but it was a good idea, Pappas. We gave it our all."

The assistant athletic director stubbed out his cigarette in an ashtray on the small desk near the door. Then he left the room.

A Hot Meal For Dinner

If Edmund Grabowski wanted one thing, it was a hot meal for dinner. But his wife Millie wasn't making it.

"You're not taking care of this house," he said.

She stood in the kitchen doorway, her hips cocked to one side, her left arm thrust across the doorway and pressing on the opposite side like a stiff baton.

"That's wrong," she said.

He shook off his jacket and let it fall on the floor and sank into the stiff chair. It was the only one they owned and sagged slightly under his weight.

"I'm right," he said. "I make the money and you cook the food and watch the children."

Millie didn't answer at first. Her index finger moved against her thumb as if she were rolling a tiny cigarette. The tip of her tongue sought the corner of her mouth as if it were seeking freedom to speak.

"You have a newborn you haven't even asked about."

"I've been busy."

"We need to pick a name."

"Okay."

"You have any names in mind?"

Edmund sighed. His dull eyes focused on the octagonal wall clock. It read four-thirty.

"It doesn't matter to me," he said. "Name her after your mother."

"We already used Isabella, you dolt. We can't do that twice."

"Then Pola," he said.

"Pola?"

"Yes."

"Like that movie star? The one carrying on with Chaplin?"

"That one."

"No, we can't."

"Why not?"

"It's not sophisticated. It sounds Polish."

"We are Polish," he said.

Millie stood there, her arm across the doorway. Behind her were the kitchen table, the oven, the cabinets.

"If there isn't going to be hot food in this house, I'm going out."

His wife's eyes blazed like hot coals. "Don't take any wooden nickels."

I won't."

Edmund picked up his coat from the floor and walked out of the house. The door slammed behind him.

A moment later, three pairs of children's eyes appeared at the edges of their bedroom doorway.

"Is it safe," one said.

"Yes," Millie said. "Now all of you children please run to the store for bread while I tend to the baby. All of you, go."

* * *

Edmund stamped down the street wreathed in fumes of anger. He stepped onto a streetcar. The sides were open for the warm June weather.

He rode the streetcar to Woodward Avenue and stepped off and moved sullenly through the crowded sidewalk. He was a hard lump in the soft flow of humanity.

A young woman dressed in a blue cloche hat and flapper dress sashayed past him with two friends, giggling. Edmund smelled gin on them and noticed their high hemlines. He turned and watched the three slim figures as they passed, and when one of them looked back at him, she giggled and clutched her friend's arm and they all walked faster away.

"Hotsy-totsy," he said, then spat on the sidewalk.

Edmund bought a ten-cent sandwich from a man at a cart and ate it while continuing down the west side of the boulevard. At the Fox Theater, he stopped under the orange marquee and thrust his hands into his pocket and found another ten cents. He gave it to the man in the glass booth and took his small ticket stub and passed inside. The plush carpet in the lobby went unnoticed under his shoes as he bought a two-cent red-and-white striped bag of popcorn from a vendor and climbed the stairs.

The balcony housed a thousand seats but they were mostly empty. Edmund selected one as far as possible from other theatergoers. He'd grown into this habit during the influenza epidemic, though he'd never worn a mask. He sat down without removing his jacket.

Below, to the left of the stage, the organist suddenly struck a chord, and the massive pipe organ issued a thunderous sound that reverberated up everybody's legs and into the seat cushions and sternums. The red curtain onstage was pulled to the sides, revealing a white screen. Edmund didn't know what story he was going to see. This was how he did it.

A newsreel began to play. This one was a Hollywood travelogue. It showed Model Ts bumping down a wide avenue. It showed a filmmaker cranking the shaft on a motion picture camera. It showed a glamorous movie premiere.

Edmund yawned.

The main picture began. It was a domestic story. Onscreen a woman with a beautiful face dressed in a long skirt was seated in a wicker chair, holding a swaddled child. Her husband in a straw boater hat and trim suit stood over her. They both looked worried.

Then a title card came up onscreen. Edmund stirred uncomfortably. He couldn't read. He'd never learned how to read in Polish either. Then the actors came back in the next scene and he relaxed.

A young man suddenly sat down in the seat next to him, tossing his coat over the back of the seats in front of them. He was wearing a casual pants and scuffed shoes and a white t-shirt with the sleeves rolled up. An anchor tattoo decorated his upper arm.

"Hi," the young man said.

Edmund stuffed some popcorn in his mouth and ignored him. Onscreen the parents were starting to cry.

"Can I have some," the young man said.

"No."

"I'm not talking about the popcorn."

Edmund turned his head. The young man had a thin lower lip and his liquid eyes were looking directly into his own. Onscreen, a doctor had arrived and was examining the swaddled baby.

"What are you doing," said Edmund.

The young man, maintaining eye contact, placed his hand on Edmund's thigh. It felt hot and soft.

Edmund glanced down at it. "You want me to break that?"

The young man pursued his lips, annoyed. He removed his hand and picked up his coat and stood up. "Don't sit at this end of the petting pantry if you can't handle the attention."

He stormed off. Edmund looked around. The other theatergoers were mostly in pairs, making out. Around him were nothing but pairs of men.

Onscreen the parents were now dressed in black, standing over a freshly dug grave, wailing in silent agony.

The organ pipes were nearly shaking the walls. The men around him had their faces pressed together. Onscreen, the mother's legs buckled, her body falling onto the earth. The others reached down to attend to her.

Edmund stood up and left the theater.

* * *

Edmund and Millie lay side by side in the dark that night. The thin mattress felt lumpy in their backs. A lit cigarette hung lazily out the side of his lip. Its orange tip was a single point in the black room.

"The baby is quiet," he said.

"Yes."

"She sleeps better than the others."

"That's true."

He looked at the bassinet on Millie's side of the bed. In

the light of the half moon, he could see the infant swaddled up in a blanket. He couldn't see her face but he thought he could see her breathing.

"When did you feed her?"

His wife made an irritated sigh. "You work and let me handle the children."

Edmund fell silent. He rubbed his foot against hers under the sheets.

"You seem well," he said.

"It's only been a week, Edmund."

"But you're up and walking."

"I am. It's easier this time."

His hand reached for hers. He rolled over towards her and tried to kiss her face. Irina grimaced and rolled away.

"No," she said.

"Why not?"

"It's only been a week."

"But you seem well."

"I'm not well enough."

He caught her by the wrist. Irina swiveled, sat up, and planted her feet on the floor.

"I have to feed the baby," she said.

He released her wrist and sank back into the pillow, one hand cast across his forehead.

"Can't she wait?"

"I told you let me handle the children."

"Go on then," Edmund said.

Millie reached into the bassinet and scooped up the swaddled mass and left the room. He stared at the ceiling until the cigarette burned down to his fingers. Then he stubbed it out in the ashtray.

* * *

Two o'clock in the morning, Edmund sat up. Next to him, the space in the bed was empty and cold. He grunted and stood up and threw his threadbare robe over his shoulders and went out of the bedroom.

At the end of the hallway a rectangle of white light sliced out from around the kitchen door. He could hear Irina weeping from behind it.

Then he saw it.

On the floor next to the kitchen door lay a swaddled bundle. It was their infant. The only explanation was that Millie hadn't had the space to lay the baby down in the kitchen. Perhaps she'd needed the counter space for cooking or baking.

Edmund bent down and picked up the infant. It felt oddly soft. He turned it around and unwrapped the face.

It was a loaf of bread.

He dropped it on the floor and straight-armed his way through the door.

In the kitchen, Millie was sitting down, hands on either side of her head. Her eyes were puffy and several balled-up tissues lay strewn about the table.

On the table lay a chafing dish. Inside the dish lay their infant. It was still and its eyes looked straight up at nothing.

"What happened?" he said.

He waited a long time as Millie made no movement to respond.

"What happened?" he repeated.

His wife sighed. "She was premature and she was sick and the doctor said she had to stay warm somehow."

"So what did you do?"

"I put her in there."

Millie inclined her head towards the oven.

"To keep her warm," said Edmund.

"Yes."

"But she died."

"Yes."

"When?"

"Tonight."

"So it didn't matter."

"No."

"What temperature did you select?"

Millie exploded. "Do I look like an idiot? Do you think I would roast a baby?"

"No, you don't."

"It was warm enough."

Edmund leaned against the wall, hands stuffed in the high pockets of his gown. He was at a loss for words. Millie's pained eyes found his and pushed them up against a wall.

"They won't bury the child unless we name it," she said.

"Pola."

"Really," she said.

"I like that name."

"I know you do."

They looked at the dead child in the dish.

"Pola is fine," said Millie.

"Okay," he said.

He picked up the blanket that the bread had been swaddled in and gently wound it around the infant's lifeless body. Then he carried it over to a grocery bag and laid the child gently inside.

"Goodbye, Pola," he said.

Getting the Axe

"These poor saps," he said.

Harry Delaney was strolling down the half-mile-long catwalk at the Rouge plant, high above the assembly line. It was barely wide enough for two to walk abreast.

His double-breasted gray suit was standard issue for the executive class, but he'd accented the outfit with a gray fedora hat, tilted stylishly to the side. On his left lapel was a small brass Rouge badge with his ID number.

Behind him walked three executives from Birmingham, England. They wore herringbone suits and banded boater hats and were midway through an eight-week tour of the United States.

"What's so poor about them?" said one of the visitors.

Delaney stopped walking and put his elbows on the railing. Below, the assembly line looked like a mural of souls trapped in eternal damnation. The small figures moved in regular patterns amid the winches, the pulleys, the sheet presses, the gears twice the diameter of a man.

"The job controls them," said Delaney. "They can't set their own pace on the line. It's very difficult."

The executives smiled in bemusement.

"We hadn't heard," said one drily.

"I understand they're paid well," said another.

"At least you get to set your own pace," said a third.

"That's right," said Delaney, "I'm very special."

This provoked laughter, so Delaney kept it going. "In fact, I often welcome very important visitors on these tours. Why, just last week I was giving a tour to the king of Sweden."

"How impressive," said one.

"We're not such small minnows ourselves," said another. "We represent BSA Limited. We produce motorcycles."

Delaney shrugged. "Our cars got twice the tires your motorbikes got, so what do you have to say to that?" He raised a playful eyebrow.

"Come now, Mister Delaney, is that any way to treat your guests?"

"Look, it doesn't really matter," Harry said. He gestured at the assembly line below. "This plant is the biggest industrial operation in the world. We're gonna keep rolling on without you, or your opinions."

There was an uncomfortable silence. "That's one reason why we're here," said another. "We were hoping to discuss striking up a partnership with the Ford Motor Company."

Delaney began walking again. The three men scurried behind, waiting for a response.

"Did you hear us?" said one.

"Yeah, I heard you," Delaney said, over his shoulder. "These are courtesy tours, not business meetings. And I doubt that your little bicycle company is listed on Henry

Ford's chalkboard of priorities. And if it is, then it would only be to buy you outright."

The three men looked worriedly at one another. "Mister Delaney, we work at BSA. Surely you've heard of us?"

"No, I haven't," he said.

"We're the largest motorcycle company in the world."

"Terrific."

"We tried to make an appointment with somebody on your executive staff, but nobody returned our messages."

"So you booked this run-of-the-mill tour thinking I was your ticket to the upper floors."

"Well, I wouldn't put it so baldly," said the British executive. "This could be a lucrative arrangement for everybody."

They'd come to the end of the catwalk. A set of stairs led down to the factory floor, and the exit doors were off to the left.

Delaney turned to face them. "I'm important here too, gentlemen. I'm somebody. The king of Sweden, remember?"

"Mister Delaney—"

He interrupted the British executive. "You can all see yourselves to the gates. Down these stairs and out that way."

He saluted the three men, then quickly descended the steps and disappeared into the steam of the factory floor.

* * *

Five pm that afternoon, Delaney stood on the carpet before Edward Stratham, the head of Ford public relations. Stratham was a thin man in his late forties with rapidly graying hair at his temples and an exasperated look in his eyes.

"It doesn't matter," Stratham said. "If someone is in a position to help Ford Motor, you send them along to Henderson on the fifth floor. No questions asked. We've been over this before."

Delaney blew frustrated air out of his mouth. "It's just a motorbike company, Edward. What's that got to do with Model Ts?"

Stratham pounded his desk. "Everything, Harry! Motorcycles have everything to do with Model Ts!"

"How?"

"They have engines! And tires! And brakes! Come on, buddy!"

Harry leaned moodily against a sideboard. He picked up a glass decanter and ran a finger down its side.

"Put that down," said Edward.

Harry set the decanter down. It wobbled unsteadily. "Surprised it's not full," said Delaney.

"It used to be."

"What happened?"

"I don't drink anymore. Also, it's been made illegal, if you haven't heard."

"The old lady finally get to ya?"

Edward squeezed the bridge of his nose between his fingers. "Sure, if that's what you wanna believe. Listen, Harry, every week it's something different with you. You were tossing candies down to the workers on one tour. On another you improvised a song-and-dance routine. Last month we found out you were telling guests that you gave a tour to the king of Sweden."

Delaney picked at his fingernail and said nothing. His Ford badge shone dully on his left lapel.

"So what are we gonna do with you?" Edward said.

"I dunno."

"You seem educated, maybe you come from some money. What do you want to do with your life?"

Delaney jammed his hands into his pockets and craned his neck downwards. He seemed to be studying his own shoes.

"I dunno," he said.

"You want to leave the plant?"

"No."

"Why not?"

"I like it here. You can't make me leave anyways." A look of infinite smugness spread across Delaney's face. "I'm protected."

Edward lost patience. "Go back to your office and do something worthwhile. Earn your paycheck."

"Only if you give me a kiss." Delaney puckered his lips.

"Out!"

"Applesauce!"

Edward looked at him dumbly. "What the deuce does that mean?"

"Figure it out."

Delaney sauntered out the door. Edward closed it behind him and watched the cloudy shape through the frosted glass until it disappeared.

Then he went over to his filing cabinet and opened one of the drawers and pulled out a bottle of whiskey and took a long pull directly from the opening.

"Idiot," he said.

* * *

Delaney sat down in his office chair. The room was smaller than a backyard privy. It held his chair, the desk, and nothing else.

He smoothed his hands across the flat surface of the desk. It was empty except for a wooden inbox and a wooden outbox. Both were empty.

He pulled open a desk drawer. Inside lay a stack of white blotter paper and a pen. He hadn't touched them in years. Then he pulled open a second drawer. It contained a pair of old globe bookends.

"Why hello. Were you always there?" he said.

Delaney shut the drawer and leaned back in his chair and kicked his feet up and steepled his hands. He pretended to be listening to somebody.

"Unfortunately you're wrong," he announced. "Wrongedy wrong wrong wrong. You will always be wrong." He paused. "Harry, we have a question. What do you really do here in this office? On this desk? What is your purpose?"

He turned his head, listening for an imaginary answer.

"The answer is that you do nothing, Harry. You are wasting your life." He lifted his eyebrows, as if waiting for an answer. "Oh, I see. The great and powerful Edsel protects you. When was the last time you spoke with him?"

He tilted his head, still listening.

"Four years. Why, Harry, it seems that he's forgotten that you exist."

Delaney ended the monologue. He abruptly stood up, snatched his hat and coat, and stormed out of his office.

* * *

On Thursday evenings, members of the third floor of the executive building at Ford Motor Company often gathered for drinks at the Detroit Athletic Club. It was an Italianate rectangular building in the middle of downtown. The club featured full athletic facilities, a pool, ballrooms, a coat room, and several guest bedrooms.

Here, on the top-floor bar of this building, cocktails had never left the menu, for it was the playground of the wealthy.

When Edward Stratham arrived, he handed his mackintosh to the girl at the coat check. Scanning the room, he found his group congregated around the far end of the long copper bar that shone pink and gold under the lights. It was a group of five suited men standing with highballs in hand.

"I see the weekly meeting of the British Plenipotentiary Society has begun without me," Edward said.

"I never know what the hell you're saying, Ed," one replied.

Edward explained. He pointed at each of the men in turn and named them, starting with himself. "Edward, Edward, Robert, William, Charles, and George. We're the kings of England."

"Not him," said William, pointing at Robert. "Robert the Bruce was a Scot who was denied the English throne."

"Shut your pie hole, Weber," said Robert.

"Is this gonna be a wingding or a history lesson?" said someone.

A Manhattan—two parts rye, one part sweet vermouth, plus bitters and a maraschino cherry—found its way into Edward's hand. "Boy, I need one of these. You'll never guess who I had to dress down today."

"Who?"

"Harry Delaney."

Groans from the entire group.

"What did he do this time?" said one.

Edward took a swallow and shook his head. "He insulted three executives from BSA Motorcycles. They complained after the tour."

"The motorcycle company?" said Charles. "They signed up for a regular tour?"

"Yeah," said Edward. "Somebody dropped the ball on that one."

"Christ."

"Anyways, Harry ends our meeting by saying he's *protected*." Edward added finger quotes around the final word.

The group went quiet. "He's right," said Charles. "He is protected."

"But how?" said Edward. "That's what I want to know."

"He's Edsel's boy," replied Weber. "They went to Hotchkiss together."

The group sipped their drinks, all six pairs of eyes nervously looking around. This was dangerous territory for conversation.

Finally Edward broke the silence. "I'm sorry for bringing this up, but why is the Ford princeling protecting that bumsnatch?"

"Maybe he's got dirt on Edsel. Something that would hurt the brand."

George shook his head no. "That doesn't wash. Edsel's a straight shooter."

"It's time somebody got rid of that clown," said William.

Charles shrugged. "Yeah, but how?"

"I don't know," said Edward.

Robert spoke for the group. "I mean, who wants to be

the bad guy and bring it up? You? You? Hell no. There's no solution."

A brunette cigarette girl came along displaying her wares on her tray.

"Evening, gentlemen," she said, "tonight we have Camels, Lucky Strikes, and Chesterfields for eight cents a pack. Is anybody interested?"

The men paused to admire her thighs beneath her short skirt and the single jaunty feather rising from the band that circled her head.

"I know what I'd like," said Robert, "but I can't quite put my finger on it."

The men laughed.

* * *

Later that night, Edward retrieved his mackintosh, tipped the coat check girl, and started for home. He was halfway down the large marble staircase to the main floor when a voice caught his ear.

"Edward!"

He turned around. The voice belonged to William Weber, leaning against one of the marble spheres at the top of the heavy balustrade railing.

"I am an old-fashioned drunk," he said, "on old-fashioned drinks."

"You need some help?" said Edward.

"Hey, listen here—I know how to do it."

"How to do what?"

"How to get rid of him."

Edward turned his head. "Delaney?"

Weber nodded. "Come here." He crooked a finger.

Edward sighed and trudged back up the marble staircase. William leaned in and whispered something in his ear.

"That's very odd," said Edward.

"But it sends a message. Doesn't it?"

Edward turned back down the stairs. "I'll have to think about it."

"Tell me how it goes." William spread his arms out wide, grinning. Then he hiccuped and stumbled back into the bar.

* * *

The waiter brought two glasses of wine to the table and set them down with a smile.

"Your usual, Mister Delaney."

"Thank you, Giovanni," said Harry.

Harry was dining at the Roma Café, in the Eastern Market. He was seated at a romantic two-top in the corner of the room, against a wall painted with an attempted representation of St. Peter's Square.

His date, a young girl with bobbed hair and a short fringed dress, sat across from him with a big grin on her face.

"Whatsa matter, toots?"

"Nothing's the matter."

"Is it the drinks? They grandfathered in an exemption here for communion wine because the owner's brother is a priest."

"Do you know everybody in this town?" Her voice sounded naive.

Harry shrugged. "I get around, I spend money, I have a good time. People know me."

"I should say so."

He lifted his glass. "To you, and to us."

"This is so exciting," she said, shimmying in her seat. They clinked glasses.

"You don't like to go out?"

"Nobody's ever taken me out," she said.

"A girl like you? I don't believe it." He lit a cigarette. "What are you, twenty-two? Twenty-three?"

"Eighteen," she said.

His face fell slightly. Then he shrugged it off and took a drag on his cigarette. "You don't look eighteen, toots."

"I have a name, you know."

"Sure you do. At least, a couple."

"What's my name, Harry?"

"Christina."

"I thought you'd forgotten."

He blew smoke at her. "I did. See, you're a good girl. All the good girls are named Christina."

She made a face and picked at the bread on the table. "I liked it when you told me the story about the king of Sweden."

"He was a nice fella," Harry said. "Say, you have a job? Or do you just get by on that pretty face?"

She lowered her eyes. "I work at the cigar factory."

"San Telmo on Dequindre?"

She nodded.

"So you're Polish."

She nodded again.

"You ever been to the Rouge?" he said.

"No."

"Would you like to go?"

"Maybe. When?"

"Tonight. What say we finish these meatball sand-wiches, get in my car and I can show you my office. We can get to know each other a little better. Maybe we'll even run into Edsel."

"Who is Edsel?"

He dropped the bomb. "The president of Ford Motor Company."

"Edsel Ford!"

"We went to school together, out on the East Coast."

Her eyes flashed with excitement. "Oooh, exciting."

Harry leaned backwards in his chair, arched backwards, and blew smoke on the back of the woman sitting behind him. She started coughing. The woman's husband started a fuss.

Harry straightened up and looked at his date. "I'm bad, aren't I?"

* * *

Edward Stratham stood the kitchen of his home, dressed in a ribbed cotton undershirt and gray slacks and slippers. A cigarette dangled from the corner of his mouth.

He was staring at the brass candlestick telephone that sat on a small mahogany table.

"Edward, the children are waiting," said his wife's voice from upstairs.

"I need a minute," he answered.

Drawing a deep breath, he pulled out the small chair at the telephone table and seated himself at it. He lifted the receiver and held it to his ear.

The young female's voice came online. "Operator, how may I connect you?"

"Ford Motor Company, Service Department," he said.

"One moment please."

He could hear the woman connecting the plug. Then he could hear the other end ringing.

"Service Department," said a gruff voice.

The operator hung up. "This is Edward Stratham, head of public relations. Who am I speaking with?"

"Joe."

"Got a last name, Joe?"

"Maybe."

Edward frowned. "Let me guess. You're Joe Citronelli. Your boss is Charlie Peterson. And Charlie's boss is the man whose name we don't speak."

There was silence. "How did you know all that?"

"Because I'm the head of public relations, you donkey."

"All right, Mister Stratham, you got me. What can I do for you?"

"I need you to do me a small favor tonight. It'll only take a few minutes."

"Sure thing, Mister Stratham."

"I have to warn you, it's a bit odd."

"How's that?"

Edward looked around and lowered his voice. "Do you think you can find an axe?"

Harry rolled into the executive office building, the girl hanging on him, giggling. One glass of wine had gone to her head.

"My heavens this place is so nice," she said, looking around.

"Yeah, you should see the dining room."

"Harry Delaney, you must make a lot of money—"

"Would you believe that I just bought an entire Caribbean island?"

Her voice went up to a screech and her mouth opened in a pantomime of disbelief. "Say, now you're pulling my leg—"

"Naw, sweetie, it was a two-for-one sale. I got the other one for you!"

She giggled. They began climbing the staircase to the third floor. Christina suddenly pushed her body against his. He felt the railing digging in his back.

"Careful there," he said.

Her eyes searched his face. She chewed on her lip daintily. "I want you to throw me across your desk."

"Funny but my desk asked me to do the same thing to you, toots."

He seized the hair at the nape of her neck and pulled her face to his. Their lips met in a violent kiss. Then she pulled away.

"My name is Christina," she said.

"Not anymore. That's for good girls only."

Harry grabbed her hand and pulled her upstairs. The long hallway was darkened. She gripped his hand, he fumbled for the key to his office.

Then he stopped.

Inside his office, the light was on. A figure was visible through the frosted window of the door. He heard the sharp sound of something cracking.

"What the—"

Delaney dropped the girl's hand and yanked open the door. Inside was a brute of a man wearing dark dungarees and a denim work coat and a scuffed black porkpie hat. In his hand hung a heavy axe.

On the floor were the pieces of what used to be Delaney's desk.

A line of sweat ran across the man's lip. He wiped it off.

"They asked me to do this," the man said. "I don't know who you are. They told me to do this."

"Who's they?" shouted Delaney.

"The Service Department."

Delaney clenched his fists and leaned back and yelled at the ceiling. It was a barbaric sound. His date cowered behind him, her hand covering her open mouth, fear in her rounded eyes.

Then he lunged for the man's axe. "Gimme that!"

"No," said the man, twisting away.

"You can't break up my desk!"

"I just did."

Delaney tried to snatch the axe out of the man's hands. Soon it was a tussle. The strange man was bigger but Delaney had the power of rage.

The two men fought with their legs intertwined, the sides of their torsos flush with one another, their hands gripping the axe.

"Let go!" shouted Delaney.

"No!"

At last Harry lost his grip, and the man stumbled backwards. He fell into the girl in the doorway and the blade of the axe sliced down her lower left calf. A sheet of flesh peeled off like a piece of lunch meat.

The girl screamed in pain and fell to the floor. Harry and the man stood there, panting, looking at her.

"What do we do?" the man said.

"I don't know!" shouted Delaney. "I'm not a doctor!"

His date was moaning on the floor, the blood seeping in

a thin sheet down her ankle and soaking her shoe. Her fingers opened and closed.

"Somebody should take her to the hospital."

"First you take off your shirt and wrap her leg in it," said Delaney.

"No, you do it!"

Delaney smacked him on the shoulder. "This is a two-hundred-dollar suit!"

The man took off his coat and stripped off his t-shirt and wrapped the girl's leg in it. The shirt turned red as the blood soaked through.

"Help me carry her out to my car."

The two men formed a chair with their arms and lifted the now-unconscious girl and ran down the hallway, down the stairs, and to Delaney's car. They placed her in the passenger seat.

Harry turned to the man. "You clean up the blood upstairs, and we say nothing of this. We didn't see each other. I was never here."

"You got it."

"Shake on it."

The men shook on it. Delaney got behind the wheel and tore off into the night.

* * *

Nine o'clock the next morning, the executive meeting was underway in an oak-lined conference room that was trying to pass itself off as a European baronial chamber. Nine men were seated around the long wooden table.

Edward Stratham sat in an armchair, fingers over his mouth, thinking quietly.

Then the door swung open. Harry Delaney hobbled in

on a pair of crutches, and his lower left foot wrapped a large white cast.

"Sorry I'm late, fellas," he said. "I had a bit of an accident last night."

The conversation paused as the eyes swung his way. "What happened?" said George.

"I got into a tussle with a streetcar," he said.

"That's some bad luck," said someone.

"Well, don't mind me," he said. "Just give me a minute to drop my things off in my office, and we can start when I come back."

Stratham's eyes widened. He shot to his feet. "Harry, don't worry about going to your office. In fact, we don't see a need for you to be here today."

"Why's that?"

"How will you be able to get around the floor with your tour group?"

Delaney looked downcast. "That's a good point, Mister Stratham. Could someone give me a ride home?"

Edward came around the table. "Why sure, I'll call one of the boys to give you a lift. No reason at all for you to be here."

Harry nodded at the executives around the table. "Gentlemen, have a good day."

Hand on his shoulder, Edward steered Delaney out of the room and into the hallway and downstairs.

Outside, he called a driver. The man pulled up and Edward helped Harry into the passenger seat. "You take a few days to recuperate," he said.

"That's awfully nice of you, Mister Stratham," he said.

"My pleasure."

The car drove off. Edward walked back into the conference room and collapsed into his chair.

"What the hell was that about?"

Edward closed his eyes. His fingers squeezed the bridge of his nose.

"Fellas," he said, "does anybody here know where we can find a new desk?"

Black Bottom

Saturday afternoon on Hastings Street, and Marvin Booker moved through the crowded sidewalk like a young shark through a school of fish.

"Lookin sharp Marvin!" said a passerby.

The compliment slid off his back. Marvin always took pride in his appearance. On this day, he'd chosen a cream shawl-collar sweater over a white collared dress shirt. From under his crisp gray slacks peeked a pair of shiny brogues that had cost him his entire paycheck. On his head was perched a stylish blue flat cap.

Other passersby nodded. He kept moving until he arrived at a corner store. The words *Stubbs' Grocery* was stenciled on the window. It was a standout, even on a bustling commercial street like this one. A stream of people poured in and out of the doors.

Marvin stepped inside. The smell of warm fruits and vegetables crept inside his nostrils. He sneezed twice.

"Bless you," said a voice.

It was the owner, Mister Stubbs, an elderly man in a pair of crisp overalls who carried himself with a no-

nonsense air of efficiency. Standing behind the counter that ran alongside the room, his veined hands planted on its smooth wooden planks, he was studying Marvin over his spectacles the way an entomologist studies a specimen.

"Thank you," said Marvin.

He felt the owner's eyes upon him as he moved through the crates of apples, the boxes of corn flakes, the bags of flour.

He picked up a small bushel of potatoes and a pack of cigarettes and returned to the counter.

"You go by the name of Booker," Mister Stubbs said.

"Yes sir."

"You have a Christian name?"

"Marvin."

"Pleasure to meet you, Marvin." He glanced down at the younger man's brogues. "You've got a healthy sense of yourself."

"Yes sir, I suppose that's right."

"How do you make your daily bread?"

"At the Rouge. I'm in the foundry."

The man's eyes widened slightly. "What you think about that?"

"There's no future in it."

Stubbs nodded. "You can try a job here for a week," he said. "I'm looking for a new stock boy."

Marvin shook his head no, his eyes searching the ceiling. "I want something really big." He spread his hands out wide, as if grasping the size of his future success.

Stubbs removed his spectacles and put one hand on his hip. A smile spread on his face. "I believe this young man is suffering from a delusion of grandeur."

"It's just that—"

The old man cut him off. "You are standing in the most

successful black-owned grocery store in the entire state of Michigan. This grocery store is the beating heart of this neighborhood. And did you know that I come to this city same way you did? A little boll weevil blown up on a cotton truck. That's facts. You hear what I'm saying?"

"Yes sir," Marvin said. "Can I pay for my things?"

Stubbs didn't break eye contact. "Forty-three cents."

Marvin left him two quarters on the counter and headed for the door. Stubbs shouted after him, "That offer still stands. One week only."

* * *

Marvin thunked his head against the streetcar window, feeling the cold predawn air against his cheek. He was dressed in faded dungarees and hobnail boots with thick soles. The heavy coat on his shoulders was stained and ripped, but his face was scrubbed clean and his liquid brown eyes had fixed themselves on something in the far distance.

Next to him, a stout young man with cheerful face was talking. His name was Harold. He and Marvin worked together at the Rouge. Though Marvin didn't know where Harold lived, they'd found themselves on the same streetcar often enough to become regular seat mates.

Harold loved talking and it didn't matter about what. He narrated life, running his mouth about every topic from women to booze to the global auto market. He knew almost nothing about everything.

It didn't matter. Marvin didn't mind the stream of soft noise that bathed his ears every morning. It brought him slowly into the day.

"—so that's when I found the store," Harold was saying,

"the one that one fella told me about, it's down on Gratiot, this man who owns it, I don't know where he come from, somewhere in Europe I think, but he sell nothin' but postcards, he selling those postcards one penny each, and people just scoopin 'em up like candies, and he don't do nothin' but put them on some shelves and stick his hand out—"

Marvin turned his head. "He makes money selling postcards?"

"—that's what I was just tellin you, this man sells postcards, named Sal or something, his store on Gratiot right down by that one park with the little fountain where that the woman died next to last month, you remember that, it's somewhere in that area, maybe at Harper, maybe a bit north, no hold on, I'm sorry, it's to the south—"

Marvin thought about this as the streetcar arrived at the plant. He stood up to leave.

"You always forget your bag," said Harold.

"Ah yeah, thanks."

Marvin slung his bag over his shoulder and marched off the streetcar.

* * *

At home that night, Marvin was heating his iron on the tiny stove while his three roommates bantered from where they lay in their bunks.

The four men all worked in the foundry and shared a two-room wooden clapboard house. They were all recent arrivals from Tennessee. Their landlord himself was an attorney from Knoxville who'd come north to invest in a small auto company. He lived with his wife on the other side of the city.

"I'on't think there's much more to it," one said. "They can't enforce shit."

"Crime is changin' man, this guy told me about it," said another.

"I heard so many things," said the third.

The first one's eyes settled on Marvin. "Hey, what you doing over there?"

Marvin was standing against the wall, arranging his pants on a wooden board. Then he went to the stovetop in the corner and used a rag to lift the hot iron off the surface. He ran the hot instrument lightly along the slacks.

"What's it look like I'm doin?" Marvin said.

"Tryin' to look prettier than the ladies."

The three men laughed.

"No," Marvin replied, "I'm preparing to make something of myself."

He lifted the slacks and affixed them to a pair of clamps mounted on the wall. Then he stepped back and admired his work. They hung down straight and proud, as if awaiting orders.

"We are looking at the next president of Ford Motor Company," said the second roommate.

The others laughed. Marvin lay face down in his bunk and put his pillow over the back of his head, wishing he could be anyplace else.

* * *

Gratiot Avenue was a mess of vehicles. Small trucks and Model As dodged one another madly, trying to overtake the large streetcars that rumbled down the middle of the street, their metal pieces clanging like a set of Chinese percussion.

Alongside the scrum, Marvin moved smoothly on foot

down the sidewalk. He'd left his umbrella at home, so he walked slowly under the store overhangs, then ran quickly between them, trying to avoid the rain.

At the corner of Gratiot and Mack, he found the store. A handwritten sign in the window read *Postcards by Sal*.

He lifted his hat off his head, held it against his chest in a sign of humility, and entered the establishment.

The store was narrow, the brown air so stuffy that breathing felt like a chore. Eight double-sided racks of postcards were arranged in a pair of rows from the front to the back. Standing near the back wall was a chubby man wearing a clean white apron around his waist. He was holding a small black receiver cupped to his ear. It was connected by a wire to a vertical cradle that stood on the table next to the till.

"Are you Sal?" said Marvin.

The man nodded and held up a finger: wait. "Connect me with the New Hellas Café," he said into the receiver. "I know it's the third time today. I know they're not picking up. No, why would I know where they are? Fine, I'll try again later. One more thing—you sound like you're fourteen years old. Oh you're sixteen, I'm sorry."

Sal replaced the receiver in the cradle and lit up a cigarette. "Don't get one of these," he said. "They're more trouble than they're worth."

"Hello," said Marvin, offering his hand, "my name is Marvin Booker, I see you sell postcards."

Sal blew a ring of smoke into the air and cocked his head, looking at the young visitor's hand. "A Negro with perfect manners."

"Yes sir."

"Don't see that every day."

Marvin withdrew his hand. "I already have a job but

I'm looking for a new occupation. I've heard that you sell postcards and that you do very well at it."

Sal crossed his arms. "Tell me why should I talk to my future competition?"

"I wouldn't open anywhere near you. I'd sell to Black Bottom."

"It's still not good business."

"It could benefit both of us. Also, I could sell postcards that you wouldn't."

"That's horsepucky."

Marvin picked up a postcard from the rack. It was a hand-drawn colorized image of Campus Martius in the center of downtown.

"People eat that one up," said Sal.

"For just one penny," said Marvin.

Sal sucked on his cigarette. "One little penny."

"How many you sell a day?"

"A couple hundred."

"I don't believe it."

Sal frowned, then stubbed out his cigarette into a small brass ashtray. "Come back here, I'll show you something."

Marvin started towards him, but Sal stopped. "Wait. Lift your arms."

The young man obeyed. Sal patted him down, his hands going along Marvin's sides, around the small of his back, inside his pockets.

"Okay," he said, "this way."

He led Marvin into the back office. It was barely big enough for two people to stand side by side. A single round light fixture dangled above a long table that was piled with stacks of new postcards. "I just got this shipment yesterday. I sell one of these every two weeks."

Marvin's eyes took it all in. "I could do this."

"Maybe. I want to see your people do better, so here's my advice. Don't start with a store."

"No?"

"Handsell the postcards in your neighborhood. Hustle after hours, on the weekends. See how it goes."

"Okay."

"If things start picking up, then you can think about this." Gus twirled his finger in the air around the store.

"Very good advice, Mister Sal."

"And," said the proprietor, "just because I'm in a generous mood, you can go ahead and take one postcard from this selection. Any one you want."

Sal beamed with pride. Marvin obediently began rifling through the stacks on the table, feeling the older Greek's eyes on his back.

"You have a girlfriend, Marvin?"

"No sir."

"Where does a young man like you find satisfaction?"

"Nowhere sir."

Sal snorted. "That's the first lie you've told."

"It's not. I just don't know where to go."

"Hattie Miller's takes Negroes."

"That so?"

"It is. You should stop in there. Tell 'em I sent you."

Marvin selected a postcard of a pine tree in front of a row of log cabins. The title read *Lone Pine Lodge*.

"That's a good one," Sal said, "but nobody wants it. I've got seven more."

"For us, a single pine tree meant it was safe to camp out on the land. Back in the old days, when we were running."

The postcard shop owner nodded. "Maybe that explains it."

"It'll sell to my people."

The shop's front door opened and the sound of young women tittering and giggling floated into their ears.

"That's my cue," said Sal. "It's time for you to leave, Marvin."

"Thank you, sir."

Marvin slipped around him, glided past the girls, and left the store.

* * *

Nighttime. Marvin checked the address that he'd written on the slip of paper. *Hattie Miller's, 165 Hastings.*

It was a turn-of-the-century house, three stories, sturdier than most. A single well-lit doorway on the ground floor illuminated a staircase that ascended to the second floor.

Marvin cleared his throat and went over to the doorway and rapped loudly. There was no response. He turned the doorknob and it opened easily. He drew a deep breath before entering.

Shutting the door behind him, he climbed the red carpeted staircase. At the top, he found himself in a red parlor with low brocade couches, floral vases, a wet bar, and an upright piano. The scent of perfume assailed his nostrils and from a spinning Victrola danced the tinny sound of a ragtime standard.

A woman sat at a small desk. She was heavy and blunt-faced and held a fountain pen in her right hand. A ledger was opened on the table before her. The room was otherwise empty except for a single whore in a lacy pink slip reclining on a nearby chaise lounge. Her skin was pale white but her eyes were hard blue marbles that had pinned themselves upon Marvin.

"Hello," said Marvin.

"We don't have any rooms tonight," the madam said.

"But it's Monday," he replied. "I came here tonight because nobody comes on Mondays."

"No," came the reply.

"What about tomorrow?"

"We're filled up," she said.

"Wednesday?"

"Same."

A cruel smile appeared on the whore's mouth.

"Sal sent me," said Marvin.

"Who?"

"The postcard guy. He said you'd take all clients."

"Oh, him," replied the woman. "Sal is a straight liar. He knows we don't take Negroes."

Marvin clenched his fist but kept his face straight. "Have a good night, ladies."

"You too," said the whore.

He turned and walked down the staircase and went out back into the night.

* * *

Two weeks later, Marvin entered his rooming house. A roommate lay in his bunk paging through a nudie magazine. The white models wore their hair short, according to the style, and their breasts fell heavily over their corsets.

A wooden crate had been placed on the floor next to Marvin's bunk.

"This better be what I ordered," he said.

"A truck brought it this afternoon," the roommate replied.

Marvin kneeled down and inspected the delivery. The top of the crate had been pried off.

"Why is it open?" he said.

The roommate set down his magazine. "I opened it to check for you that it was all there."

"Is it?"

"Yeah."

Marvin looked inside. There were several packs of fifty postcards, each wrapped in brown paper. Marvin began removing the packs, one by one, from the crate. He lined the packs neatly on the floor, then counted them.

"There's only nineteen. I paid for twenty."

He looked over. The roommate reached under his pillow and pulled out the twentieth pack. He tossed it at Marvin.

"You buy your own," Marvin said. Then he hit the roommate in the foot.

* * *

At five o'clock the next morning, Marvin posted himself near one of the gates of the Rouge. A bag was slung around his shoulder. In his left hand an array of colorful postcards was fanned out.

As the workers poured out of each streetcar and moved towards the gate, he began his spiel. "Postcards, one cent, postcards, one cent, six for a nickel, bright colors, parks, skylines, nightclubs, send them home to your friends and family, postcards, one cent, postcards—"

After an hour, Marvin stuffed the remaining postcards in his bag and counted his money. He'd earned thirty-six cents.

* * *

The Rouge boasted more than forty entry gates, and Marvin sold postcards in front of a different gate every morning. After three weeks, he'd sold nearly seven hundred, netting him almost seven dollars.

"That's a three-and-a-half dollar profit," he said to Harold.

They were sitting on the streetcar, going home. Marvin opened his bag and showed his seat mate the postcards and the small purse of money. Then he closed the bag and put it on the floor.

Harold shrugged. "That's how much you make in five hours in the foundry."

"I know. But if I can grow this, I don't have to work in the foundry." He leaned over and pulled the cord.

"Those postcards," said Harold, "ain't nobody want postcards anymore, used to be that a postcard meant something, now they just get chucked in the trash or the fireplace, these days everybody wants a phone call, but have you ever tried to use one of those telephones, it takes forever to connect and—"

"Sweet Jesus," said Marvin, "this is finally my stop. Harold, you talk too much. Anybody ever tell you that?"

He stood up and stepped off the streetcar and disappeared down the street. Harold looked down at the floor.

"You left your bag," Harold said.

* * *

Next morning, Marvin scanned the faces anxiously on every passing streetcar.

"Come on, Harold," he said.

Five, ten, fifteen cars passed. There was no sign of him. Marvin checked the clock in the window of a nearby business. It was already six-twenty. He was going to be late.

Sighing, he boarded the next streetcar and took a seat alone.

* * *

The streetcar arrived at the Rouge precisely thirty-five minutes later. As he stepped into the foundry, his foreman shouted at him.

"Booker, over here."

The foreman was a strong white man with a gruff attitude. "Let's get to the point. You're not working here anymore."

"Did I get promoted?"

"No, you got yourself fired."

Marvin froze in his shoes. "For what reason?"

"You've been selling those postcards outside the gate every morning. Management doesn't like it."

"There's no law against it."

"No, but management doesn't like it."

"I don't get a warning?" Marvin replied. "I can stop."

The supervisor jerked a thumb over his shoulder. "Out. Go open your own business."

Marvin turned. A guard at the door motioned outside with his head. His right hand patted his baton.

Clenching his jaw shut, Marvin trudged out of the foundry.

* * *

Seven thirty pm. Next to the light of a simple lamp, Mister Stubbs peered over his spectacles, studying the ledger of the week's sales. His pencil was squeezed tightly between the tips of his fingers.

The tiny sound of a chime sounded, and the front door opened.

"We're closed," he said without looking up.

"I'm here about that job," said a voice.

The elderly proprietor looked up. "Marvin Booker," he said.

"You remember my name."

"I see you've decided to listen to the gospel of stability."

"I got fired from the Rouge. And my postcards got stolen."

"What position did you come here to claim?"

Marvin took his hat off and held it against his chest. "Any position you think I'm worthy for, sir."

"My offer expired two weeks ago, captain."

Marvin nodded. "You are a successful business owner. I'm humbly asking that you show me what you know."

Mister Stubbs set down his pencil. He came around the counter. "Go over to that aisle and let me watch you stack and arrange the creamed spinach."

"Yes sir."

Marvin found the cans in a crate on the floor. He quickly formed a row of towers four cans high, then turned each can so its label faced outwards.

"All right," said Mister Stubbs. "You come back tomorrow morning, I'll give you a try."

"Thank you, sir."

"Standard clothing. No greasy overalls, no suit. I want to see a plain collar shirt and slacks."

"Yes, sir."

* * *

The typhoid scourge began nine days later. In the first wave, eighteen people died and hundreds were sickened. Across the city, people threw out their fresh food, scrubbed their sheets, pulled lice from their children's heads.

The rumor mill started up. It reported that the epidemic had begun with the chickens at Mister Stubbs' grocery. In response, Mister Stubbs had pointed out that his chickens were purchased from a purveyor who also sold them to twelve other groceries. This fell on deaf ears.

The first brick came through the window at eight thirty-two on a Tuesday morning. Marvin was badly shaken but unhurt. Mister Stubbs was in the back room when it occurred.

At ten-seventeen that morning, the first looter broke down the front door. He met a premature death from a rifle that was fired by Mister Stubbs. He was seventeen years old.

At ten forty-nine that morning, the second looter broke into the grocery store. He met the same premature death from the same rifle, also fired by Mister Stubbs. He was twenty-two years old.

At ten fifty-three that morning, a group of fourteen looters rushed into the store. The rifle was seized, and Mister Stubbs was knocked unconscious with its butt.

During the melee, Marvin Booker was stabbed in the hands, wrist, shoulder, bicep, and groin. The coroner later wrote in his report that the wounds had been consistent with self-defense. He was twenty-four years old.

I'm the Pony

In the booth, Charles Stitch wiped the sweat off his upper lip as he took another bite of his ham sandwich.

His wife Martha was across from him, dressed plainly, a plate of eggs before her. Their five-year-old daughter Lily fidgeted next to her. She wore a simple light blue cotton dress for traveling, and a straw cloche hat with a matching blue silk band. In the crook of her arm was a small home-made toy pony made of brown cloth.

Charles held out half of the sandwich to his little girl. "Are you sure you don't want any, sweetpea?"

Lily shook her head. "I'm not hungry."

"You don't want anything?"

"Not here, this place smells funny."

Martha looked at her husband, confused. "I don't smell anything, do you?"

He shrugged no. "She's got a good nose. All I know is, we can get there by three pm if we eat quick."

"Did you hear that, sweetie?" said Martha, patting Lily's leg. "Only three more hours!"

"I don't like the automobile," the girl said in her piping high voice.

"But that's where your daddy works. He makes the cars!"

Her eyes went wide. "He builds the cars?"

"I work at Ford," Charles said, "in the public relations department." He swallowed and pointed outside with his fork. "And that Model A outside makes everything possible. Your clothing, your food—even that pony."

She ignored him. "I want to ride a pony," said Lily, gazing into her toy's eyes.

"I don't think they have ponies where we're going," said her mother.

"Hey sweetpea, do you know what we're going to do when we arrive?" said Charles. "We're going swimming in the *lake*."

Lily pinched her lips together and lifted her face. "But is it dangerous to go swimming in the lake?"

"No, it's not," said Charles.

"Do you think that ponies go swimming?"

"That's a good question," said Martha, "and maybe daddy can answer it later."

Charles exchanged glances with Martha, then rose from the booth. Lily had been talking about ponies for almost four months straight. There was no getting her off the topic.

He paid the bill at the cash register, adding a bag of six molasses cookies to take on the road.

* * *

The Stitch family stepped out onto the sidewalk. They were in Standish, Michigan, a small transit town about a hundred and fifty miles north of the city of Detroit.

They'd left their home at seven o'clock that morning with one steamer trunk of clothes strapped to the rear end. This particular restaurant was named Wheeler's, a new roadside diner that had sprung up just a few months before on US-23. It was aimed at capturing some of the new automobile traffic coming up from downstate in the summers.

Charles slid behind the wheel of the family's new Deluxe Roadster. Martha helped Lily reluctantly climb into the rumble seat, then seated herself in the passenger seat.

"This bench hurts," Lily complained.

"Impossible," said Charles, "this Model A is the pride of the nation. Nobody else makes automobiles like this."

"Can we put the roof down?" said Lily.

"If you put the top down," said Charles, "you won't be able to see all the wild ponies."

Martha smiled warmly at him. Charles checked the parking brake, inserted the key, turned the gas valve three-quarters of a turn counterclockwise, pulled down on the throttle lever a few clicks, and pushed on the starter pedal. He waited for the motor to crank through a couple revolutions, then pushed the choke back in. Finally, he turned the gas adjusting valve back down, so the engine wouldn't be flooded with fuel.

"We are ready," he said.

He popped the clutch and pulled onto the two-lane road and pointed the car northwards.

* * *

The automobile passed through the cornfields, the tassels and the green silks swaying in the summer sunshine. The aroma of loamy soil floated through their noses. Next to him, Martha held her hat onto her head with her left hand and gazed out at the passing farmland.

"It's beautiful," she said. "I wonder who lives here."

"Only the farmers, maybe a few Amish."

"Is that so?"

She patted the side of the vehicle. "They won't like to see us coming in this, will they?"

He laughed. "Speaking of which, dearie, did you bring the whiskey?"

"We didn't have any."

"Oh."

"Is that a problem?"

"No," he said, "it's probably better to leave it back in the city anyways. Up here, they're different."

"These Protestants don't take kindly to imbibing," she said, deepening her voice in a mocking tone.

He matched her tone. "This country is being ruined by the party of rum, Romanism—"

"—and hellions!" Martha leaped on her husband and buried her face in his neck.

He laughed. "Get off, I am driving—"

"I know!"

The car swerved before he could gain control of it. Martha pulled back, her eyes full of fun and playfulness.

"Be good," he said, wagging a finger.

She snapped her teeth at him.

Behind them, Lily flew her toy pony in figure eights through the air.

* * *

At five o'clock that night, Charles emerged from the waters of Lake Huron. He was wearing his simple black swim trunks and slicking his hair back with his hands. Behind him were six small wooden-log cottages. Their Model A was parked in front of one.

Martha came to the edge of the water and stood next to him, looking out. She was wearing a Jantzen suit, which was a black tank top sewn to a pair of black swim shorts. It was the newest fashion.

"This lake looks lovely," she said, letting the small waves touch her toes, "but oh! much too cold."

"You'll grow used to it." Charles sized up his wife in her swimsuit. "My oh my, how daring. What would Caroline say?"

Martha blushed. "My mother would kill me."

"Without a doubt."

"I wouldn't dare wear this back home."

"But here, you're free." Charles placed his hands on his hips and looked around. "Where's Lily?"

They both turned. Their daughter was running under the pine trees that bordered the property, her toy pony held sky high. She was talking to herself.

"She's got a bright future in flying pony sales, that's for sure," he said.

His wife was looking at him mischievously. "Charles."

"What?"

"We need to celebrate our arrival."

"Okay."

She raised an eyebrow. He caught her meaning. "Right now?"

"Lily seems occupied for now. And there's a lock on the door."

"You checked."

"Of course."

"Then by all means," he said.

The couple joined hands and went back to their small cottage.

* * *

The couple were under the sheets in the cabin when a knocking sounded at the door.

"Let it be," said Charles, pinning down Martha's arms.

"No," said his wife, "it could be Lily."

"It's surely not."

"But it could be."

"She'll survive—"

With effort, Martha heaved her husband off her. "Just one minute," she said.

Charles fell back on the bed and pulled the sheet up around him and covered his eyes with his forearm.

Martha wrapped herself in a robe and walked over to the door and opened it.

It was Lily.

"I have something to say," she said, striding into the cabin.

Charles sat up in bed. "What is it, sweetpea?"

Lily took a deep breath. Then she shouted, "I FOUND A PONY!!!"

Charles and his wife exchanged glances. Martha was the first to speak. "Where is this pony, Lily?"

"I don't knooooow!" she said.

"Well how do you know there is a pony?" said her father.

"Because I found its *footprint*!"

Lily stamped her little foot on the floor. She was the very picture of certainty.

"You found a pony's footprint?"

"I did!"

"Sweetpea," said Charles, "why don't you give mommy and daddy a few minutes and we'll meet you outside."

"But I want to show you *now*!"

He sighed. Martha bent over and kissed her daughter on the head. "Just let me get dressed and you can show me what you found."

Charles blew air out of his mouth. He should've brought whiskey.

* * *

A few minutes later, dressed in a bathrobe, Charles let his daughter drag him by the hand to a patch of ground near the pines. His wife was already standing over it.

A cigarette hung from the corner of his mouth as he peered down. "Well, I'll be damned."

In the dirt was the impression of a horse's cloven footprint. It was somewhat circular, with a large left and a large right toe separated by a triangle of space in the middle.

"I told you!" she screamed.

"What do you want to do with this?" he said.

"I want to find the pony!"

He smiled. "Well, which way did it go?"

"This way!"

Lily ran a few feet away. Her parents followed. Sure enough was another footprint.

"There's more over there," said Martha.

"And even more over there!" shouted Charles.

"Oh this is fun!" said Martha. "Don't you think this is fun, Charles?"

"Great fun," he said, puffing on the cigarette.

Lily grabbed her hand. "Come on," she said, "let's go!"

"Aren't you coming?" said Martha to her husband. "We need to find out where it leads."

"Have at it," said Charles, gesturing towards the road. "Let me know how far they go."

He blew a kiss and walked back towards the cabin.

* * *

Eight pm. The family sat in a circle on the bed, cross-legged, eating cold potato salad and fried chicken.

"Tell me what you found one more time," said Charles.

"Hundreds of pony prints!" shouted Lily.

"—without shouting," he said.

Martha used a napkin to wipe fried chicken from her daughter's cheeks. "She's right though, dear. The hoofmarks went all the way to the road."

"And," said Lily, "and then and then we went across the road and found the pony walked that way into the forest—"

"We don't know that for sure," said Martha.

"There were more pony prints on the other side of the road?" said Charles.

His wife nodded. "They went down a trail. They're very faint."

The little girl was bouncing on the bed now. "It's a *secret* trail! Can we go down the secret trail tomorrow? Can we?"

Martha took her by the hand and guided Lily back down to a sitting position. "Calm down, that's enough, Lily."

"We had plans tomorrow," said Charles. "We were going to lay on the beach and play in the water."

"I don't care about the water," said Lily, "I just want to find the *pony*!"

"Your opinion has been noted," he said.

The little girl flopped backwards on the bed. "I'm never going to sleep tonight."

* * *

Later, in the stillness of the night, Lily ran through the cabin, flying her toy pony through the darkened air.

In the bed, Charles and Martha lay side by side, wide awake, eyes staring at the ceiling.

Martha rolled over and whispered into her husband's ear.

"I think you're going to have to change those plans for tomorrow."

* * *

In the morning, Charles and Martha followed their daughter down the narrow forest path. The trail was covered in soft pine needles the color of copper. The sweet smell of pine resin encircled their heads.

In front of them marched little Lily, striding loudly, talking to herself the whole way.

"There's another one!" she shouted. "Number seventy-three!"

"That's number seventy-three!" said Charles. "What do you think, dear? Will there be a seventy-four?"

Martha grasped his hand and smiled. "She's going to remember this day for a long time."

"Especially," he replied, "when she can't find the pony and it ruins the entire vacation."

The family moved through sun-dappled forest. Flies at

their ears. Mushrooms growing at the base of the trees. Prehistoric ferns flowering from the forest floor.

"How long have we been walking?" Martha said.

Charles looked up at the sun peering through the canopy. "Nearly an hour. We must be three miles off the road by now. And she's still going."

They listened to Lily's small singsong voice filling the forest as she entertained a thousand different stories about what happened to the pony.

Martha laughed. "I think she's on a mission from God."

"Isn't that the truth," he said.

"I smell something," Lily announced.

"A lot of pine sap," said Charles. "It's everywhere. Look, Daddy got some on his hand."

She ignored him. "It smells like *sugar*."

Martha inhaled deeply. "I don't smell anything. Do you?"

"It's the aroma of her own obsession," her father said.

"Look!" Lily shouted. "I see them! Very clear!"

Ahead, the hoofprints tracked through the mud in the middle of the trail. They extended straight down the trail to a bend in the forest.

"We're following you, kid," said her father.

"Charles, look," said Martha.

She was pointing up ahead. There was an olive tent that hung from a line strung between two trees. Next to it, a skinny man stood pissing, his back to them, one hand leaning against the tree trunk.

"Sweetpea, come here, quickly," said Charles.

He ran forward and scooped the little girl up and passed her to Martha. They stopped walking. The pissing man had heard their commotion and zipped up and turned around. He wore blue dungarees and a loose white shirt and red suspenders. On his feet were odd black boots. A salt-and-pepper beard clung to his face like a frightened forest creature.

In his hand hung a shotgun.

"Hallo there," said Charles, "sorry to disturb you."

"What do you need?" the skinny man said.

Charles winced. The man's body odor was palpable from thirty feet away.

"Nothing," he said, palms raised.

The forest dweller tilted his head. "How you come to arrive here?"

"On the trail," Charles answered, "my daughter wanted to explore. We're staying at the cabins a few miles back."

"We're following the pony!" shouted Lily. Martha immediately shushed her daughter.

Charles grinned. "Never mind her. Have a great day. We'll be going back now."

The man's eyes narrowed. He was watching Lily. "Hold up. That girl say you all followin' a *pony*?"

"That's right."

"I know where that pony is."

Lily erupted into a cheer. Martha clapped her hand over her daughter's mouth.

"Oh yeah? Where's that?" said Charles.

"Right around this bend." His thin arm pointed around the curve of the trail ahead.

"Is that so?"

"Yes sir. Go on up the trail a bit more and you'll find him."

Lily was staring rapt at the man. "What does he look like?"

"I reckon you'll recognize him. There's only one pony here."

The family didn't move. The skinny man followed Charles' eyes down to the weapon in his hands.

"I ain't gonna hurt you," he said.

"I don't know that."

The man threw the shot gun into the forest. "Go on now. You'll see him. He's right there."

Charles and Martha looked at one another. He lifted an eyebrow. She shrugged.

They resumed walking down the trail. The skinny man stepped aside as they passed. The scent of his body odor was mixed with the scent of whiskey. He'd been drinking all by himself, out here in the pine forest.

"Thank you," shouted Lily.

His strange eyes fixed on her own as she passed. Martha turned her daughter's face away.

Charles walked backwards, keeping an eye on the man. The tent dweller stood in the middle of the trail, watching them oddly.

"Let's hurry," Martha whispered.

"Yes."

They turned the bend in the trail and found themselves in a clearing in the forest. In the middle stood an open-sided structure. Four thick pine trunks served as posts, holding up a flat pine roof that was covered by a black tarp.

Under the flat pine roof was a sealed pot, four feet high, with a tube leading out of its cover into a cylindrical iron tank sitting nearby. A wreath of orange flames licked out from beneath the pot. Something inside was boiling.

"That's what I smelled!" shouted Lily.

"Look over there," said Martha. On the edge of the clearing were four crates of empty green bottles, at least a hundred total.

"Oh my Lord," he said.

Martha set Lily down on the ground but gripped her hand. Her eyes found the contraption under the roof. "Charles, what is that?"

"We have discovered an illegal whiskey-making operation."

"That's a pot still," she said.

"Yes."

"I've never seen one before. What does this mean?"

Charles blew air out of his mouth. "It means this strange feller is in bed with some ugly people."

Martha looked at her husband. "Organized crime."

"Yes."

"We shouldn't be here."

"No, we shouldn't."

They stood, their feet anchored to the ground, unsure of what to do next. That's when they heard it.

The sound of heavy galloping coming out of the forest behind them.

"It's the pony!" Lily shouted.

They whirled. Bursting around the bend of the trail was the skinny forest-dwelling man. A cotton bag made to look like a donkey's head had been draped over his own, with eyeholes cut out. A rope had been looped loosely around his neck and dangled down his chest. His feet were beating a strange loping rhythm on the ground.

And he was running straight for them.

The parents stood tightly together, clutching Lily to their knees.

"Stay away!" Charles shouted, holding one arm up.

"I'm the pony!" the man shouted, "I'm the pony!"

"It's the PONY!" shouted Lily.

The man ran past the family and galloped in a lazy

circle nearby. "Look down!" he shouted. "Look at the ground! I'm the pony! Do you see it!"

"Oh my heavens," said Martha. "Charles, look at the tracks he's leaving on the ground."

Charles finally saw it. The man's black shoes weren't ordinary shoes. Strange clogs had been affixed to the soles.

They were leaving horse prints on the ground.

"You really are the pony," Charles said.

The man slowed to a walk, then stopped. Through the bag, he said: "You got it, bub."

The forest-dweller bent over, hands on his knees, catching his breath. Then he straightened up and removed the bag from his head. His crazy eyes and salt-and-pepper beard seemed to be more alive than before.

"What in blazes are you up to out here?" Charles said. "Humans aren't meant to live all alone like this."

"Ain't no humans up here!" the man said. "Just us ponies!" He laughed maniacally. Lily began giggling.

"I am quite confused," said Martha.

"He wears those pony print shoes so nobody knows he's out here," said Charles. "To evade the Prohibition Bureau."

"I'm speechless," said Martha, staring at the man. Then she lowered her voice: "He is also quite drunk."

"That is certain."

The man wiped his nose on his sleeve, then sat down cross-legged in the mud.

"This is our time to go," said Charles. To the man: "You have a calm and reflective day, sir."

"Bye, pony," said Lily.

He waved sadly at her.

Charles picked up Lily, threw her over his shoulder, and grabbed Martha by the hand. Then they began to run back down the trail.

* * *

An hour later, they were back at the cabin. Charles began loading up the Model A.

"So we're leaving?" said Martha. "Just like that?"

"I got to swim, you got to wear your swimsuit, Lily got her pony, and we met a madman in the woods who's cooking an illegal substance and knows that we know about it. The week is complete."

Lily tugged at his pants. "Can we come back next year, Daddy?"

He kissed her on the head. "Most certainly not, sweetpea."

Thank you for reading!

Visit Plotworks Publishing to sign up for our newsletter and to purchase more titles by J.A. Jernay, A.J. Renwick, and others.

Now turn the page for a free sample of *The Hardy Boys: The Tower Treasure*, by Franklin W. Dixon.

THE ILLUSTRATED

HARDY
BOYS

THE
TOWER
TREASURE

book
1

FRANKLIN W. DIXON

The Tower Treasure: Chapter 2

The auto brakes squealed.

The driver of the oncoming car swung the wheel viciously about. For a moment it appeared that the wheels would not respond. Then they gripped the gravel and the automobile swerved, then shot past.

Bits of sand and gravel were flung about the two boys as they crouched by their motorcycles at the edge of the embankment. 'The car had missed them only by inches!

Frank caught a glimpse of the driver, who turned about at that moment and, in spite of the speed at which the automobile was traveling and in spite of the perils of the road, shouted something they could not catch at them and shook his fist.

The car was traveling at too great a speed to enable the lad to distinguish the driver's features, but he saw that the man was hatless and that he had a shock of red hair blowing in the wind.

Then the automobile disappeared from sight around the curve ahead, roaring away in a cloud of dust.

"The road hog!" gasped Joe, as soon as he had recovered from his surprise.

"He must be crazy!" Frank exclaimed angrily. "Why, he might have pushed us both right over the embankment!"

"At the rate he was going I don't think he cared whether he ran any one down or not." Both boys were justifiably angry. On such a narrow, treacherous road there was danger enough when an automobile passed them traveling at even a reasonable speed, but the reckless and insane driving of the red-headed motorist was nothing short of criminal.

"If we ever catch up to him I'm going to give him a piece of my mind!" declared Krank. "Not content with almost running us down he had to shake his fist at us."

"Road hog!" muttered Joe again. "Jail is too good for the likes of him. If it was only his own life he endangered it wouldn't be so bad. Good thing we only had motorcycles. If we had been in another car there would have been a smash-up, sure."

The boys resumed their journey and by the time they had reached the curve ahead that enabled them to see the village of Willowville lying in a little valley along the bay beneath them, there was no trace of the reckless motorist.

Frank delivered the legal papers his father had given to him, and then the boys had the rest of the day to themselves.

"It's too early to go back to Bayport just now," he said to Joe. "What say we go out and visit Chet Morton?"

"Good idea," agreed Joe. "He has often asked us to come out and see him."

Chet Morton was a school chum of the Hardy boys. His father was a real estate dealer with an office in Bayport, but the family lived in the country, about a mile from the city. Although Willowville was some distance away, the boys knew of a road that would take them across country to the

Morton home, and from there they could return to Bayport. It would make their journey longer, but they would have the pleasure of visiting their chum. Chet was a great favorite with all the boys, not the least of the reasons for his popularity being the fact that he had a roadster of his own, in which he drove to school every day and with which he was very generous in giving rides to his friends after school hours.

The Hardy boys drove along the country, roads in the spring sunlight, enjoying the freedom of their holiday as only boys can. When they had reached a culvert not far from the Morton place Frank suddenly brought his motorcycle to a stop and peered down into a clump of bushes in the deep ditch.

"Somebody's had a spill," he remarked.

Down in the bushes lay an upturned automobile. The car was a total wreck, and lay bottom upward, a mass of tangled junk.

"Must have been hitting an awful clip to crumple up like that," Joe commented. "Perhaps there's someone underneath. Let's go and see."

The boys left their motorcycles by the road and went down to the wrecked car. But there was no sign of either driver or passengers.

"If anyone was hurt they've been taken away by now. Probably this wreck is a day or so old," said Frank. "Let's go. We can't do any good here."

They left the wreckage and returned to the road again, resuming their journey.

"I thought at first it might be our red-headed speed fiend," said Frank. "If it was, he was sure lucky to get out of it alive."

The boys gave little further thought to the incident and

before long they were in sight of the Mortons' house, a big, homelike, rambling old farmhouse with an apple orchard at the rear. When the boys drove down the lane they saw a figure awaiting them at the barnyard gate.

"That's Chet," said Frank. "I'm glad we found him at home. I thought he might have gone out in the car."

"It is strange," Joe agreed. "On a holiday like this he doesn't usually stay around the farm."

As they approached, they saw Chet leave the gate and come down the lane to meet them. Chet was one of the most popular boys at the Bayport high school, one reason for his popularity being his unfailing good nature and his ability to see fun in almost everything. He was full of jokes and good humor and was rarely seen without a smile on his plump, freckled face.

But today the Hardy boys saw that there was something wrong. Chet's face had an anxious expression, and as they brought their motorcycles to a stop they saw that their chum's usually cheery face was clouded.

"What's the matter?" asked Frank, as their friend hastened up to them.

"You're just in time," replied Chet hurriedly. "You didn't meet a fellow driving my roadster, did you?"

The brothers looked at each other blankly.

"Your roadster? We'd recognize it anywhere. No, we didn't see it," said Joe. "What's happened?"

"It's been stolen."

"Stolen?"

"An auto thief stole it from the garage not half an hour ago. He just went in as cool as you please and made away with the car. The hired man saw the roadster disappearing down the lane, but he supposed I was in it so he didn't think anything of it. Then he saw me out in the yard a little while later, so he got suspicious—and the roadster was gone."

"Wasn't it locked?"

"That's the strange part of it. The car was locked, although the garage door was open. I can't see how he got away with it."

"A professional job," commented Frank. "These auto thieves always carry scores of keys with them. But we're losing time here. The only thing is to set out in pursuit and to notify the police. The hired man didn't see which way the fellow went, did he?"

"No."

"There is only the one road, and we didn't meet him, so he must have taken the turning to the right at the end of the lane."

"We'll chase him," said Joe. "Climb onto my bike, Chet. We'll get the thief yet."

"Wait a minute," cried Frank suddenly. "I have an idea! Joe, do you remember that car we saw wrecked in the bushes?"

"Sure."

"Perhaps the driver stole the first automobile he could lay his hands on after the wreck."

"What wreck was that?" asked Chet.

The Hardy boys told him of the wrecked ear they had found by the roadside. It had occurred to Frank that perhaps the smash-up might have occurred just a short while before and that the driver of the wrecked ear had resumed his interrupted journey in a stolen automobile.

"It sounds reasonable," said Chet. "Let's go and take a look at this wreck. We can get the license number and that may help us find the name of the owner."

The motorcycles roared as the three chums set out back

along the road toward the place where the upturned automobile had been seen among the bushes. The boys lost no time in reaching the place, for they realized that every second was precious and that the longer they delayed the greater was the advantage to the car thief.

The car had not been disturbed and apparently no one had been near it since the boys had discovered the wreck. They parked their motorcycles by the roadside and again went down into the bushes to examine the wrecked car.

To their disappointment the car bore no license plates.

"That looks suspicious," said Frank.

"It's more than suspicious," said Joe, who had withdrawn a little to one side and was examining the automobile from the rear. "Don't you remember seeing this car before, Frank. It didn't occur to me until you mentioned the matter of license plates."

"I have been wondering if this isn't the same car that passed us on the shore road at the curve," replied Frank slowly.

"It is the same car. There's no doubt of it in my mind. It didn't have a license plate, I noticed at the time, for I wanted to get the fellow's number. And it was a touring car of the same make as this."

"You're right, Joe. There's no mistake. The red-headed driver came to grief in the ditch, just as we said he would, and then he went on to the nearest farmhouse, which happened to be Chet's place, and stole the first car he saw."

"The busted car was the one the fellow was running who nearly sent us over the cliff," Joe declared. "And it's ten chances to one that he's the fellow who stole Chet's roadster. And he's red-headed. We have those clues, anyway."

"And he went on past our farmhouse instead of turning back the way he came," cried Chet. "Come on, fellows—

let's get after him! There was only a little bit of gas in the roadster anyway. Perhaps he's stalled by this time."

Thrilling with the excitement of a chase, the boys clambered back onto the motorcycles and within a few moments a cloud of dust rose from the road as the Hardy boys and Chet Morton set out in swift pursuit of the red-headed automobile thief.

Plotworks Publishing

Buy the fully illustrated version of this classic 1927 boys' adventure novel at Plotworks Publishing. Available in both electronic and paper versions!